For my dear ones,
Abby and Kyle, who make it all matter

Other Books by David Scott Milton

The Fat Lady Sings
Skyline
Kabbalah
Paradise Road
The Quarterback

ISBN: 978-0-9836329-2-4

Library of Congress Control Number: 2011930616

Editor, Christopher Meeks

Book Design, Kiran Sethi & Pranay Desai

Published by White Whisker Books, Los Angeles, 2011

IRON CITY

DAVID SCOTT MILTON

Chapter One

It felt like rain. The sky was leaden, the air thick and damp. The cab ride in from the airport seemed interminable. The air conditioning was not working. Kalinyak's suit had soaked through with perspiration. He felt tired and sticky and uncomfortable. Since I've been gone, he was thinking, I've lost my tolerance for humidity.

The road in from Pittsburgh International was ragged with new construction. There were potholes and wooden barriers and great chunks of asphalt torn up. A thick tangle of trees rose in a fierce angle to one side of the road: locust and sumac, oak, buckeye and tamarack. Mount Washington, with its serpentine cobblestones streets and clapboard homes, loomed before him, a steep escarpment cascading with green. He noticed drizzle leaching from the tree leaves, the ground dark, wet loam. The air had a musty smell thick as syrup.

He had been living in the desert west so long, he had forgotten how lush and green this part of the country was.

"Where you from?" the cabbie said as though reading his mind. A large man in his sixties, the cabbie rasped through a hunk of black, rope-like stogie, a Marsh Wheeling.

"Tucson."

"Hot there. Cactus and stuff, right?"

"Oh, yeah."

They drove through a long tunnel, "The Tubes" Pittsburghers called them, and came out on Liberty Avenue. Downtown rose before them, crisp and clean even under a dark, cloudy sky. He was surprised how pristine the city was now, how brilliant, rich with color. His memories of growing up here were suffused in gray. His childhood was gray with grit and soot. Of course, he thought. All the heavy industry had died, the steel mills, the Bessemer converters, the blast furnaces.

They crossed a river, the Monongahela. All along it, the steel mills, which had once bloomed with such furious energy, were either dead or gone. Only a few rusting and blackened skeletons of mills remained. The riverbanks, which at one time had throbbed with power, blast furnaces spewing fire and smoke high into the sky, were now eerily placid.

"Business?"

"Reunion."

"Oh, yeah. Been bringing them in all weekend." He was driving through downtown now. "Never been to one. What for? So everyone can see what a failure I am?"

"I don't know about that..."

"Let me tell you. I was forced to give up one of them good steel union mill jobs. In them days, hourly was anywheres from fifteen to twenty bucks. You had your quarterly profit sharing based on earnings per ton."

"Earnings per ton—"

"Not to mention cost-of-living protection, your health and safety provisions, pension—"

"Pension? Right."

They pulled up to the hotel. Kalinyak paid the cabbie, lifted his suitcase from the trunk, and entered.

It was an old hotel, the Forrest Harris, in the heart of the downtown section. At one time, it had been the luxury hotel of the city. Still nice, it had a wide marble lobby, thick red carpeting, ornate brass balustrades. A hotel chain had bought it and made it accessible to the middle-classes.

There was a sign in the lobby: "Saturday, August 30, 7:00 PM. Taylor Allderdice Class of 1966. Thirty Year Reunion." He looked around to see if he could recognize anyone from his class. The desk clerk was young, blonde, and attractive. "Reservation. Francis Kalinyak." She barely acknowledged him. That's the trouble when you're middle-aged, he was thinking: where once women found you charming, they now look at you and they don't see you at all, and they can't wait till you're gone. They look at you like you're an asshole.

The room was spacious and modern with a great, large king-size bed. The hotel chain had obviously renovated all the rooms. He sat on the edge of the bed. He felt heavy. Everything about him felt heavy. He gazed at himself in the mirrored sliding closet door. He had gained weight in recent years. Too much sitting around staring at the wall or television, too much junk food and pizza.

At one time, he had been fast. Oh, yes, *fast!* Power thrills, but speed kills. In his days as a prize-fighter he had been known as "Hurricane." Now he was, what? Not even a tepid breeze. He could feel the heaviness in his legs, in his stomach, in his soul. To look at me, he was thinking, you would say there's a man of middle years in reasonably good shape, husky rather than fat, but he knew in the way he moved how far out of shape he was.

Age was gaining on him. No matter how fast he tried to run, the years pulled him back. The old great black baseball player Satchel Paige had said, *Don't look back, something might be gaining on you.* All he ever seemed to do was look back.

His life was that road retreating in the rear-view mirror.

He studied himself in the sliding closet door mirror. He gazed at himself with what he felt was a certain objectivity. He was beginning to look like his father. That was the truth of it, and it made him shudder inside.

His close-cropped hair was graying, but his moustache was dark. Interesting. Hair on top turning white, eyebrows, moustache black. Why? If you could figure out what caused it, you could make a million dollars, he was thinking. Get rid of all the hair dyes. You take a pill once a month—no more gray. *Gray Away,* he would call it.

He wondered how women saw him now. In his youth, he had done all right. Now? Obviously the desk clerk hadn't been impressed. He stood up before the mirror, threw a few punches, bobbed, weaved.

He took off his suit coat and trousers and stood before the mirror in his underwear and shadow boxed. Outside the hotel, it had begun to rain. It hit the window glass in great, thick splats. He heard a loud crack of thunder. He stood at the window and watched the rain. Jagged shards of lightning cracked off the high building tops. It was pouring now, and it felt fresh and good.

He unpacked and showered, shaved, brushed his teeth. He had four hours until the reunion. Who would be there, he wondered? Would he know them, would they know him?

Bobby Mack would be there, and he looked forward to seeing him after all these years. Bobby Mack had located him: how he had done it, Kalinyak wasn't sure. Bobby, who worked in the Pittsburgh D.A.'s office, had his sources, no doubt. He considered it. How much did Bobby know about him, about these last years?

Bobby had begged him to come. "Jack Dahlgren's dead. Murdered."

Their old friend, Jack Dahlgren, one of the original five Huns of the Mirror Street Aces. It had happened a few weeks earlier, mid-August.

In hearing about it, Frank Kalinyak hadn't been surprised. No, the surprise was that it hadn't happened years before. It had been predictable from their youth. Had there been a category in their senior high school journal, "Most

Likely To Be Murdered," Jack Dahlgren would have won hands down.

"I learned you're retired," Bobby had said.

"They forced me out."

"That's what I heard. I may have a deal for you. Come to the reunion. Do you have the fare?"

"As long as the airlines take plastic."

"We'll reimburse you," Bobby Mack had said. "Keep all your receipts."

"We all have our fates to live out," Frank Kalinyak now said aloud. He thought about Jack Dahlgren and the Five Huns and the old days, and he was filled with despair, a dull ache, a deep, yawning ache, a toothache of the soul.

What was he doing here, he was thinking? He had no place else to go. That was the gray, dispiriting truth of it. His life had hit a dead end. He realized this and it was not a good thought. He was going through the motions. He was not interested in these people, his old high school chums. He wasn't even particularly interested in Jack Dahlgren, finding out who killed him, except in a clinical, empty way. He was going through it because he had nothing else to do. And he was a professional.

Dealing with murder had been his life, his bread and butter, the old dog and pony show; he had been a cop for so many years, in homicide for much of that time. *"There's been a murder." "Hand me the yellow crime site tape... Who done it? Could be this one, could be that. Gimme a beer..."* Yes, the old dog and pony show, a workhorse plodding along.

He was haunted. Ghosts. They came to him unannounced, rose up in his consciousness. He forced them down, buried them, buried the past. It was the only way he could live.

These people, his old classmates, didn't interest him, Pittsburgh didn't interest him. Nothing interested him. He only knew the dull ache of unbearable loss that rested in the center of his soul...

He took out of his suitcase five framed photographs of a young girl. He set them about the room. He gazed at them and he fought not to weep. "You're with me wherever I go," he whispered. He kissed one of the framed photos, a picture of the girl in a garden. She stood sad-faced among the flowers.

She would come to him in dreams. It was this picture alive. He could smell the flowers. He tried to make her laugh. He could never succeed.

The phone rang, Bobby Mack: "Okay, good. You're here. I was afraid maybe at the last minute..."

"I figured, why not? What else do I have to do?"

"I'm glad you came. I would have never gone to this thing if I didn't know you were going to be here."

"I been thinking about Jack Dahlgren," Kalinyak said.

"You don't know the half of it," said Bobby Mack. "Look, my office is in walking distance. Why don't I come by for a drink? I'll fill you in."

"What're you doing working today? It's a holiday."

"Use the week-ends to catch up. No rest for the weary. I'll meet you in the lounge downstairs."

* * *

Kalinyak sat at the bar off the lobby sipping a Diet Coke. There was a silver dish of cocktail mix, peanuts and pretzels, and he struggled not to eat them. He was the only patron in the bar. The bartender, who had asked for his order in a light Irish accent, busied himself cutting thin slices of lemon peel.

In the mirror behind the bar, Kalinyak saw a very large man, heavy set, with a great shock of white hair moving toward him. He was grinning broadly. "This is the reason I'm here!" Bobby Mack called out. They embraced. "I would have recognized you anywhere."

"I thought you were your dad," Kalinyak said. "You used to be skinny as a twig."

"I don't deprive myself. Why? What's the sense? Hey, I'm buying. Give the good man another," he called to the bartender.

"Diet Coke."

"What's that about? Glenlivet for me," he told he bartender. "No ice."

"It had me by the balls and I didn't like the feeling. Been off the sauce six years now."

"Jesus, what's the use of living?" Bobby Mack took a pack of Camels from his suit jacket and offered one to Kalinyak.

"Gave 'em up, too," Kalinyak said.

"Really? I admire you for that. I've tried. Jesus knows how hard I've tried."

"I lost my marriage behind the booze. Figure if I'm going to give up the booze may as well give up the smokes."

"Lost your marriage over it? Me, too. Your wife was - I met her long time ago—"

"Rita."

"That's right. Not a Greenfield girl—"

"South Side."

"Had a Polack name, as I recall."

"Schmidt."

"Schmidt? What kind of Polack name is that?"

"Family was German. Migrated to Hungary. Old man came here to work in the mills."

"Didn't they all."

"So with the booze and all, we both blew it. She could put it away as good as the next guy."

"That was after—"

"About a year."

"I heard what happened. I don't know how a person lives through that."

"I'm not sure I did live through it," Kalinyak said with a wan smile. "Here's a picture..."

He opened his wallet and displayed a picture of the young girl whose framed photos he had set about the hotel room. She was eight years old, standing in a flower bed, with a sad, lost smile. "Beautiful," Bobby Mack said.

"She was everything to me."

"Crying shame," Bobby Mack said. "And they never found—?"

"Naw, didn't have a clue. Oh, they looked, they looked high and low all right. After all, I was one of theirs. The department was on it morning, noon, and night. They just never quit. Could have been anybody."

"How'd it happen?" Bobby Mack puffed on his cigarette, coughed. Frank Kalinyak did not speak for a while. "You don't have to talk about it."

"No, it's good that I talk about it. It's hard, but it's good. She was in the backyard, playing. My wife was right inside the house. I was working. It was two in the afternoon on a Saturday. Someone came in the yard and just took her and drove her out into the desert and raped and killed her. Eight years old."

"Mother of Jesus..."

"Not a clue. Nothing. This was before DNA, but even years later, the DNA brought up nothing. Could have been— anybody. Oh, they hauled in every pervert they could find. Nothing. It destroyed me, Bobby. I don't want to burden you. It destroyed me. You remember me from the old days. I could take care of myself."

"Oh, yeah."

"But this—?"

"I understand."

"I felt it was some kind of retribution..."

"For what?"

Kalinyak didn't speak. He stared in the ice in his glass. "Well," he said at last. "It had a great effect on me, Bobby."

"I can understand."

"I was always tough on rapists and child molesters, when I came across them. After this—well, I should have retired for my own good."

"You busted some people up?"

"That's what they said. They said I busted a lot of people up. So tell me about you, about your job. You never became District Attorney?"

"Never wanted it. I'm happy just doing my work, hired hand. These days, I don't even do much courtroom stuff. I'm more or less the man behind the scenes. I got twenty years in now. I could retire. I'm not about to do it. So they severed you?"

"Yeah. I was drinking heavily. Punched the living shit out of one guy too many. They gave me my walking papers."

"You earning a living?"

"I work for some bail bonds guys. I do some PI work. I keep busy."

"And women?"

"Since my divorce, I haven't been doing much in that area. It makes it tough when you don't have money. Who's going to go for a guy forty-eight years old and he's scraping by? I have a fling every once in a while, but nothing to write home about."

"Hey! Hey!" a voice shouted to them. "Where are those Huns? Rape and pillage!" A large balding man in a seersucker suit accompanied by a dumpy middle-aged woman was moving toward their table. "Here they are! Two of them. Two of the Five Goddamn Huns!"

"Who is it?" Bobby Mack said.

"Tino..."

"Tino Bronk? No shit!" Bobby Mack said. "You got old..."

"This is, I'd recognize him anywhere, The Hunky Hurricane! Kalinyak! Haven't changed—well, a little gray... And this guy—"

"I got gray, too," Bobby Mack said.

"You know how I know it's you? Tino said. "You look just like Big Greenfield Bobby now. Spitting image. How is your father?"

"Been dead now ten years at least. Hey, the way the man drank, it's a miracle he made it that long. This is—"

"My wife. Stachursky. Kitty. Remember, from over on Loretta Street? Her brother was Gold Hat."

"Gold Hat? Jesus," Kalinyak said. "Gold Hat Stachursky. Whew. Name from the past. And Kitty. I remember Kitty. You were in class with Betty Malloy."

"We were good friends. She married—"

"Would you believe that?" Tino said.

"What?" Kalinyak said.

"Jack Dahlgren."

Kalinyak exhaled and shook his head. "Betty Malloy with Jack Dahlgren. That's a shocker. I would have never figured that."

"You were sweet on her," said Kitty Stachursky Bronk.

"Oh, that was, what?" Bobby Mack said. "You kids must have been in eighth grade."

"She had a crush on you," Kitty said. "All the girls had a crush on you."

Kalinyak smiled wanly and sighed. "Tino, where you live now?"

"I'm up in Detroit," Tino said.

"He works for Ford."

"Good," Bobby Mack said.

"Oh, it is good. You got your benefits there, you got union protection and all," Tino said. "I was working there for J&L. No more. Good riddance. What do you think? How many of the Mirror Street Aces are going to be here tonight?"

"How many are still alive?"

"Only Dahlgren is dead, far as I know," said Bobby Mack.

Tino and his wife stood uncomfortably for a long moment. They were both smiling. "This thing with Jack Dahlgren," Tino said, shaking his head. "He was an asshole, always was, but who could have figured this?"

"He was *our* asshole," Bobby Mack said.

"I was very shocked," his wife said, tsking. They lapsed into silence. Bobby Mack swished an ice cube around in his mouth.

"Hey, we'll see you tonight!" Tino stood beaming at the two of them. "Look at yuns! Just look at yuns!"

"Yuns look good," Kitty said. "Believe me, Frank, you still got it..."

"I been trying like hell to get rid of it!" he said. They all laughed.

Kitty and Tino moved off.

"So what happened with Dahlgren?" Kalinyak said.

"This is very complicated. Tonight, we'll enjoy the reunion. Tomorrow, I'll take you over the office and we'll go over things."

"Was it ugly?"

"That it was. Someone carved him up. Big time."

"Whoa."

"He had fucked a lot of people. He did some unscrupulous things, bad things."

"Like what?"

"You mean for a living? First it was siding, then he got into some other hustles. He was legitimate. But you can be legitimate, more or less, and fuck up a lot of people. That's what he did."

"Were you guys friends?"

"With Jack, he had no friends. You know that. He could be friendly with you, but not friends."

"Married Betty Malloy?" Kalinyak shook his head.

"Lasted, oh, a good dozen years. Woman is a saint to last that long with Jack Dahlgren."

"I always liked her. Good kid."

"Still is. I see her regularly. She works for Doyle the Egg. She's a legal secretary."

"Doyle Eggerman. What's he up to?"

"Don't worry about Doyle. He hit it very big. Married Kari Grace. You remember Kari, beautiful, rich. Grace Trucking. Got all their legal business, owns a chunk of the company. The father died you know, and Kari and her brothers, they got that whole thing."

"You know this stuff?"

"Hey, working downtown thirty years almost. Working for the county. I've seen it all."

The dish of cocktail mix on the table, which Kalinyak had been fighting to resist at last won out: he took a handful of peanuts and pretzels and began nibbling on them. "And Dahlgren, how'd it come about?"

"Very complicated."

"Business?"

Bobby Mack grimaced, shook his head. He drained his drink. He stood up. "There are things about him, none of us ever knew. So what do you think?"

"About what?"

"Is this something would interest you?"

"Why not?" Kalinyak said, not really believing it. "For old times sake."

"That's what I figure."

"Doesn't surprise me," Kalinyak said. "I mean, what was Jack Dahlgren best at? Fucking people. You fuck enough people, someone's going to fuck with you."

"Oh, someone fucked with him all right, big time. Cut him like he was a piece of sushi. The problem is probably a thousand people wanted to kill him. But I think we can do something here for old times sake. You're a pro. A pro does what he has to do."

"It'll keep me out of trouble, keep me moving, keep the circulation going."

"That's the thing! One foot ahead of the other. The way of the pro. You find your path." Bobby Mack smiled and hugged Kalinyak around the shoulders; he began to sing in a pleasant baritone: *Should auld acquaintance be forgot? And never brought to mind? Should auld acquaintance be forgot? And days of Auld lang syne...*

"Sweet Bobby Mack choir boy voice," Kalinyak said

"I'll see you tonight."

Back in his room, Kalinyak lay on the bed. He stared at the pictures of his daughter. It was still raining outside, a soft, steady rain. There was an occasional low rumble of thunder. He fell asleep and dreamed of her as he always did.

He slept for an hour and woke feeling drained. He showered again and dressed. He put on his suit and felt uneasy, dissatisfied. He should have bought a new suit for the occasion. Fuck it, he said. He popped a stick of Dentyne chewing gum in his mouth and left the room.

A half dozen people waited for the elevator, and he studied them, and they studied him, and he didn't recognize any of them. The elevator arrived, and there were more people inside, and Kalinyak felt embarrassed and uneasy. Fortunately, everyone knew someone and they went on with each other and left Kalinyak alone.

At the lobby, they all poured out, babbling and laughing and ooing and ahing. Kalinyak crossed the marble lobby and entered the main ball room, an immense high-ceilinged room that spoke of the hotel's earlier grandeur: towering marble columns, great, dazzling crystal chandelier. And all about, taped to columns, tacked to walls, green and white crepe streamers, Allderdice Dragon banners, antique "Class of '66" photos—cheerleaders, football players, grinning, goofing teen-agers—and one huge, solemn green and white placard proclaiming the Taylor Allderdice motto: "Know. Do. Be."

Kalinyak looked at it and thought, feeling a great emptiness, *I didn't know, I never did, and what does "be" mean?*

On a stage at the far end of the ballroom, a five-piece combo: accordion, bass, keyboard, saxophone, drums identified in neon and spangles on the wall behind as James Young and the Immortal Ones, plodded through a lugubrious version of the old rock number, "Book of Love." A half dozen couples, middle-aged and lumpy, dragged about the dance area in front of James Young and the Immortal Ones.

A woman asked Kalinyak his name and affixed a tag on his suit lapel. It had a picture of him as he had been in high school, taken from the yearbook. "You don't remember me?" she said.

"Oh, sure." He strained to see her nametag. It read, "Janet Palmer." He remembered the name, but could find no resemblance to either the girl in his mind's eye or the girl in the picture. "You look terrific," he said, forcing a smile. He wandered into the room.

A heavy-set, stooped man wearing very thick glasses came up close to him and studied his name tag. "Kalinyak? Didn't we have wood shop together, tenth grade?"

"I believe we did."

The man put out his hand. "Jerry Porter."

"You haven't changed so much," said Kalinyak.

"I had a stroke."

"No! Well..."

He motioned to a heavy-set woman standing a few feet from him. "This is my wife. This is Frank."

"Hello," the heavy-set woman said without smiling.

"We had wood shop together. Mr. Jackson," the man said. "I made a pair of bookends."

"That's right. You did," said Kalinyak. "Have you seen Bobby Mack?"

"I see him all the time. I work on Smithfield Street."

"I meant tonight."

"He's here somewhere."

"Come over here, you big hunky!" A well-dressed, beefy man with an attractive woman was waving at him.

Kalinyak was startled. He thought it was Jack Dahlgren come back to life. "Who is it?"

"Don Smith!"

"Jesus," Kalinyak said. "I thought for a second you were Jack Dahlgren..."

"Thanks for nothing."

"They always used to say that about you," the woman with Don Smith said.

"Well, I never appreciated it. I was never a fan of his."

"It's the vein in your forehead," the woman said.

"In a certain light," Don Smith said.

Kalinyak laughed. "Jack Dahlgren and his vein."

"And his underwear used to get caught in his butt crack," Don Smith said. "When we were playing baseball he'd have to dig it out after every pitch. He was the pitcher. After every pitch he'd have to dig in there and free his underwear. It was a pisser..."

"You're Frank Kalinyak," the woman with Don Smith said. "You were one of the Mirror Street Aces..."

"This is Delores, my wife. She went to Schenley."

"Donny's always talking about the Mirror Street Aces. You were one of what they called the Five Huns..."

"Oh, yeah."

"I always wondered where that came from," Don Smith's wife said.

"History class, eighth grade, and Miss Beachler was teaching about the Huns and the Tartars, and we called ourselves the Huns, some of us, and some Squirrel Hill kids called themselves the Tartars. Well, our team was already the Mirror Street Aces, so five of us became the Huns—"

"You've heard of the Four Horsemen of Notre Dame?" Don Smith said. "Well, we had the Five Huns of Greenfield.

There was Frankie—he was a left halfback, there was Dahlgren, quarterback, had a helleva an arm, Bobby Mack, a fullback, wingback was Gus Magoczy—"

"And Doyle Eggerman was the wide end," said Kalinyak. "Five Huns..."

"Yuns guys was tough," said Don Smith. "Doyle Eggerman. We used to call him the Egg. Richer'n shit now. You thought I was Dahlgren?"

"He was on my mind is all." Kalinyak was thinking, it's going to be this way for the whole reunion, Dahlgren this, Dahlgren that. Even in death, Jack Dahlgren would dominate everything.

Don Smith leaned close to Kalinyak. "From what I hear he had it coming," he said quietly. "No disrespect, you know what a mean? He always was a prick, though."

And I'm going to be hunting for his killer, Kalinyak thought. Would Dahlgren ever do something like this for me? "Hey, there's Bobby now," Frank said.

Bobby Mack, looking very snazzy in a dark blue pinstripe suit, was making his way toward them. A youngish woman with very close-cropped blonde hair was with him. Her breasts seemed poised to leap out of her silk dress top.

"This is the guy I came here for!" Bobby Mack said, throwing his arm around Kalinyak. "This is Teresa McGinnis. She's not my wife. I'm through having wives. Just got rid of my fourth."

"And good riddance," Delores Smith said. "I never wanted to say anything, but that was a trashy woman." Teresa McGinnis' light blue eyes narrowed and she looked away. "Did you ever know her?"

"Who?" Teresa said.

"Bobby's ex—She was my hair-dresser. Florence. Trash."

"Teresa's a manicurist," Bobby Mack said.

"Well, at least you keep it in the beauty line," Don Smith said.

Tino Bronk and a large man wearing a canary yellow suit joined them. He weighed well over three hundred pounds and the woman with him looked like a small bird next to him. "Buddha!" Bobby Mack said.

"Who's this?" the large man said, eyeing Kalinyak. "Kalin? Is this you?"

"Buddha Kruisper!"

The big man hugged Kalinyak to him. "Look at you, Frankie. Look at you!"

"You didn't lose any weight," Kalinyak said.

"What for?" said Buddha. "The more I lose, the more I gain. You remember Lorene, don't you?"

"You're in law enforcement," Lorene said. "Tucson? Right?"

"I'm retired from that."

A tall, tanned, lean man in a tuxedo approached them. He was smiling broadly. Next to him was an attractive woman, dripping diamonds. "I want to sue!" Buddha yelled out.

"I take the case," the tall man said.

"A case of scotch," Bobby Mack said.

"Doyle..." Kalinyak said.

"How've you been Frank?"

"Can't complain."

"Do you remember Kari?"

"Grace Trucking..." Kalinyak said.

She smiled a dazzling smile. "Some memory, Frank," Kari said.

"We were just counting up the Huns," Delores Smith said.

"There was Frank and Bobby Mack and me," Doyle Eggerman said. "And Gus Magoczy-- we called him Magpie. One more."

"Dahlgren," Buddha said.

"The unkindliest Hun of all," said Doyle.

"Rape and pillage," Buddha said.

"He was the only one who took that seriously," said Doyle.

"Well, you've done a little pillaging," Bobby Mack said.

"We've all done some pillaging," Doyle said.

"Not Frank. Frank was John Law. He was there to stop the pillaging..."

"Where's Magoczy?" Kalinyak said.

"You didn't know about Gus?" Tino said. "He went apeshit— oh, years ago."

Buddha began to laugh. "He became a priest! Father Gus!"

"Dahlgren fucked with him so much it just drove him over the edge," Tino said. "Became a bad lush just after we got out of school. Went up to Clarion to play football and they eventually threw him off the team. Whenever I'd see him he'd go on and on about Dahlgren. Dahlgren caused it. And then, the next thing I knew, he was at St. Vincent's. In the seminary."

"I remember when we were at St. Philomena's, I don't know nine or ten," Kalinyak said. "Magoczy—Magpie-- used to try to get the shiniest penny to put on the collection plate. He used to polish them over and over. He thought that was going to get him to heaven. He wanted to be a priest even then."

"I remember when Sarah Jo Kaczmarek was going to be a nun," Tino Bronk said.

"Whatever became of her?" Kalinyak said.

"You know, I don't know," said Bobby Mack. "I used to, you know; she also went, she went down the tubes, you know, and, when I was doing my early work with the District Attorney's office, she was in and out of trouble... I would see her— Before that, when I was a public defender and I would—she—she got into problems, prostitution, drugs.

"I heard something about that," Tino Bronk said.

"Had a bastard son," Bobby Mack said. "Left school, really went bad."

"I heard about this," Tino said. "Beautiful girl. Who would have figured that?"

"Got to figure she's been dead a good number of years," Bobby Mack said. "Never hear nothing about her."

"You feel bad, you know?" Kalinyak said.

Bobby Mack shrugged. "Oh, yeah, well, you know. Things happen when you're kids."

"Yeah, but you feel real bad."

"Hey, it was in her cards, you know," Bobby Mack said, draining his glass. "That's the way she was."

"Who was that priest at St. Philomena's Gus Magoczy really admired?" Frank Kalinyak said.

"That was Father Stan," Tino said.

"Father Stan!" Kalinyak said.

"Coached us in baseball, football. Sure," Bobby Mack said. "One big, tough guy! Whenever Gus would have a problem, he'd go to St. Philomena's to pray, and Father Stan would talk to him. You know, Gus's father left that family when he was very young. Father Stan was the man who straightened him out. He was the one who got him into St. Vincent's Seminary, and that's how he became a priest. You know, in the priesthood, you need a rabbi."

Tino Bronk laughed at that and everyone else laughed, too. Bobby Mack went on: "You know when you were in the police force, you needed a rabbi, right—"

"Rabbi," said Don Smith. "I thought yuns was all good Catholics?"

"That's what they call them," Bobby Mack said. "Someone to take care of you. Mentor. Patron. Well, in the priesthood, you need a rabbi, too. Father Stan was Magpie's rabbi..."

"Stan the Man," said Tino Bronk and they all laughed and laughed.

"Anybody talk to Magpie about the reunion?" Kalinyak said.

"I called him," Bobby Mack said. "He has an old church up near Altoona, Tracyville. He wants nothing to do with Allderdice. I told him Jack Dahlgren was dead. He knew about it; he read about it. He told me Dahlgren was the devil."

"He was," Doyle Eggerman said. "No doubt."

Buddha said, "That St. Philomena's thing messed Gus up."

"Frank, you heard about St. Philomena's?" Don Smith said

"What?"

"The church there. She's no more."

"No!"

"That was after you left," Buddha Kruisper said. "St. Philomena. She's no longer a saint..."

"No, no," said Doyle. "She was *never* desanctified. Liturgical directive. They dropped her from the liturgical calendar."

"Calendar of saints. Same thing," said Buddha.

"They make such a big deal over this. Everyone," Doyle Eggerman said.

"You're a lawyer. You're paid to quibble. Majority of people, parishioners, were upset, felt she was somehow a fraud. Stopped supporting the church."

"Whole thing collapsed. A mess," Tino Bronk said. "Some people tried to preserve the church—others said, hey, she's not a saint anymore, I'm not giving no more money—"

"Gus took it very hard," Buddha said.

"Made a big deal out of the thing," Bobby Mack said.

"Upshot, Frank, was, they sold the church—" said Tino Bronk.

"Who?"

"Complicated. The Jews have it now. Isn't that a bitch?"

"No big deal," Bobby Mack said. "Forget it."

"Someone made a bundle," said Buddha.

"Forget it..."

"No more St. Philomena's," Kalinyak said. "That's a shock."

"That's life," Bobby Mack said. "No one says it always has to be one thing or the other."

"Amen," said Doyle. He made the sign of the cross and everyone laughed.

James Young and the Immortal Ones struck up the school alma mater. People began to sing: "To Allderdice, a song of joy we sing..." and Doyle Eggerman excused himself and started for the stage. "He's the chairman," Kari said.

James Young, thick and balding, the keyboardist and lead singer, introduced Doyle and handed him the microphone. Doyle welcomed everyone, introduced the reunion committee; Sally Forrestal, who was the committee secretary, said a few words, and then they ate Chicken Kiev or Roast Beef. After, they sang songs and danced, and had prizes for the class mate with the most children, the most married, the most divorced; who had the most hair, who the least. They had a moment of silence for classmates who had died. When Jack Dahlgren's name was mentioned, it received a smattering of applause. Bobby Mack leaned close to Kalinyak, laughing. "You see, give people what they want..."

Everyone but Kalinyak was a little drunk. Bobby Mack had the most to drink, but he carried it well. The Mirror Street Aces got together and began to argue a football game with the Squirrel Hill Tartars which had been played thirty years earlier. "We were on the three yard-line," Tino said. "Frank got the ball and started around the right end."

"No, no," Bobby Mack said. "Jack Dahlgren had the ball. He was supposed to pitch it to Frank."

"Pass it to me," Eggerman said.

"Yes!" said Buddha. "He was supposed to pass it to Doyle. Shovel pass..."

"I had pulled on the play..."

"Right!" said Buddha.

"He laterailed it. Gus Magoczy picked it up, threw it to Frank..."

"I don't remember," said Kalinyak.

Lorene, Buddha's wife said, "I always heard that he threw it to Doyle."

"Yes," said Doyle. "I was on the one-yard line..."

"Dahlgren started throwing punches!" Bobby Mack said.

"That I remember!" said Kalinyak.

"He was hitting guys left and right. There was this guy, Spungen for the Tartars—"

"No, Miller!" said Tino. "It was Miller. He clocked Dahlgren. Knocked out two teeth."

"Doyle scored. It was the winning touchdown. Last play of the game," Buddha said.

"How old were you guys?" Bobby Mack's girl friend said.

"Fourteen," said Bobby.

"You didn't have much of a life even then," she said. And everyone laughed.

"I'm sure it was Frankie scored," Tino said. "I'm sure."

"I don't remember," Kalinyak said.

"If you would have scored," Buddha said, "you would have remembered."

"I propose a toast to Jack Dahlgren," said Doyle.

"You hated his guts," said his wife.

"I did. Everybody did. But he's gone. And he leaves a gap in our lives. To Jack, a son of a bitch, but our son of a bitch!" They all drank and Kalinyak took a last swallow of his watery Diet Coke.

Kalinyak talked to as many people as he could. Some he remembered, many he couldn't. A few had somehow known about his daughter, and they asked him about it, and he said as little as he could about it. Jack Dahlgren and the Five Huns were a favorite subject of conversation. He nodded and shrugged and tried to act pleasant, but he was tired and depressed and sorry he had come here. As the evening wound down, he and Bobby Mack and Bobby Mack's girl had a nightcap in the bar-- Bobby Mack and the girl, scotch, Kalinyak, Diet Coke. Doyle and his wife stopped by to say good night. "Tomorrow night, you'll come to the house," Doyle said. "We're getting as many of the Mirror Street Aces over as possible. You know where it is," he said to Bobby Mack.

"Woodbine Road," Bobby Mack said.

"Biggest house there," Doyle said.

"Whew," Kalinyak said. "Biggest house on Woodbine? You're talking the high rent district there..."

"I'm rich, Frank," Doyle said with a slight smile and his wife laughed and Bobby Mack laughed even louder. They moved off.

Bobby Mack and his girl were very drunk now. "Fucking Jack Dahlgren," Bobby Mack said.

"Will you shut up about him," Teresa said.

"He was a friend," Bobby Mack said.

"He was an asshole."

"Have it your way."

"Frank, wasn't he an asshole?"

"He was—complex..."

"You don't know the half of it," Bobby Mack said. He stood. He swayed, waving his drink around. "But I've known him since he was this big—" Bobby gestured at a figure at the height of his knees. "We're going to find his killer. It's the right thing to do. As far as I always knew you, Frankie, you were always about doing the right thing."

"But you know when my little girl was killed, it extinguished a certain light inside me."

"How could it be otherwise?" said Bobby Mack. "I understand this. We're going to resurrect the light. It's like when you were fighting. You fought that Polack, Nooky Padolsky, South Side Market Place. He had you in the corner kicking the living shite out of you. Frankie Kalin's not going down, I told everybody! I *knew* you were not going down. And you ended up blasting him a new asshole," said Bobby Mack. "Right there under his chin."

"Asshole under his chin," Teresa McGinnis said dully.

Kalinyak demonstrated. "Body first. Wham! Right by the liver there—"

"Paralyzes you..."

"Wham!"

"I knew it was a sure thing because Kalinyak never quits. You had that light inside you, that Hunky Hurricane light, burning hot and bright inside you. You wouldn't go down."

"It was a different time."

"We're going to do this for Greenfield Bobby Mack, my father. For Auld Lang Syne. My father always liked Dahlgren."

"Greenfield Bobby Mack! Some piece of work," Kalinyak said.

"From a different era. Tough as nails. And Dahlgren, a throwback. Fuck that guy before he fucks you. Olden days. That's when he had those gang-bangs and stuff. "

"Yeah."

"We all grew out of that stuff. Not Jackie, though. And we're going to find his killer. For Auld Lang Syne."

"Let's go," said Teresa.

"Jack Dahlgren deserves the effort," said Bobby Mack.

"He deserves shit! How many times did he insult you, just since I've known you?"

"You forgive people—"

"I never forgive and I never forget," Teresa said.

The two started off, arguing. Bobby Mack turned back to Kalinyak. "Tomorrow, early afternoon. I'll call you."

Kalinyak took the elevator up to his room. He entered, thinking it had been a grave mistake coming back here. But what else did he have in his life these days?

It was still raining heavily outside. The rain lashed the window. He stared at his reflection in the glass. He turned to the pictures of his dead daughter. "I miss you," he said aloud. "Nothing is worth anything without you."

He began to think of the past, of many things, of ghosts. And he pushed it all down.

He was thinking it was a good thing they had made him turn in his service revolver. Well, he couldn't have brought it on the plane. He didn't want it. He was certain that if he had it here, now, he would put a bullet in his brain.

Chapter Two

|||

Kalinyak had been up since dawn. It was still raining outside. He stood at the window and watched the rain. Bobby Mack called him early, before eight.

The morning was always bad for him. He would awaken with a feeling of dread, over what he had no idea. Sometimes it would be a dream, fragmented, never wholly coherent, sometimes his little girl would be standing at the foot of the bed, staring at him. Sometimes it would be a room in which a terrible crime had occurred, a motel room or the back of a car. A song would be playing. He would know it in the dream, but when he got up, he had lost the memory of it.

This morning he had been dreaming about his daughter. He thought he heard her calling to him, and that's what had brought him upright in the bed with a jolt. He looked at her pictures, and, for an instant, they seemed alive.

Bobby Mack picked him up outside the hotel at nine. The rain had slowed, but it was still falling. "Phil Hanratty, Deputy D.A., Homicide, is going to meet us for breakfast." He grinned. "I'm his rabbi."

"He kisses your ass."

"Avidly."

They drove through downtown to Market Square. Bobby parked his car just down the block from Johnny McGuire's Tavern. "I hate this piece of shit," he said. "Department car. They get them from the long-term pound." They hurried through the rain to the place.

Hanratty was waiting for them in a booth at the rear of the tavern. It was long and narrow, dimly lit, a long bar, a lot of dark wood. He had a tall scotch, neat, in front of him. Kalinyak had the feeling it wasn't the first of the morning. Bobby Mack ordered a scotch, also. "What you going to have, Frank?"

"I'll have coffee and a couple of eggs."

"What the hell's that?" Hanratty said.

"He's off the sauce."

"I heard you had some trouble out in, where is it?"

"Tucson," Bobby Mack said.

"Here's the thing. Bobby wants you on this thing, special investigator, like that. I'm all right with it, but I want to make it clear—you work for Bobby. Leave me out of this."

Bobby Mack laughed. "What?" Hanratty said. "This son of a bitch, politically he's iron-clad. No one can touch him. Not even Kholparis, the D.A. Not even the fucking mayor."

"I'm bullet-proof in this town."

"Well what the fuck, your father *was* the Democratic Party," Hanratty said. "If you hadn't been such a major asshole, you could have made something of yourself."

"It was my wives done it to me," Bobby Mack said, laughing.

"Kholparis?" Kalinyak said. "Spud?"

"The son. Spiro the Second."

"Time flies. Spud's son? Wow."

"Oh, sure, times flies. Bet on that." Hanratty said.

Kalinyak's eggs and sausage arrived. Hanratty and Mack had steak and eggs. "So, there's a lot of delicacy about this thing, which is why I'm putting it in Bobby's hands."

"What's so delicate?"

Hanratty looked at Bobby Mack.

"Jack Dahlgren was in bed with everyone," Bobby Mack said, "in more ways than one. That's why, to be honest with you, no one gives a shit if they find out who killed him or not. That's just the way it is."

"To be honest with yuns," Hanratty said. "I'm surprised you're making this effort."

"I want to light the old fire here with Kalinyak," Bobby Mack said.

"That's noble," Hanratty said.

"I'll be honest with both of you. There's not much fire left, if anything." Kalinyak regretted now having come this distance. He felt embarrassed in front of Hanratty. He remembered him from the old days. He was a hell of an athlete-- baseball, football, basketball. He played for Peabody High, and they had competed many times. He must think I'm a real loser now, Kalinyak was thinking, taking charity from Bobby Mack.

Seeing all his high school friends, his old teammates and opponents, filled him with a kind of desperate gloom. Where was his life now? What did he have to show for anything? Maybe if he could discover who killed Jack Dahlgren, that would give him something.

"This friend of yours, Dahlgren. He was a piece of work. Yuns two went way back with him..."

"I remember in second grade, St. Philomena's Sister Mary Bertha's class," Kalinyak said. "And Dahlgren was behind me hitting the back of my head, and I kept telling him cut it out and he wouldn't stop, and finally I just wheeled around and belted him right in the mouth. I think I knocked out two of his teeth, fortunately baby teeth. But he never forgot that. Years later, when we were adults, he exploded at me one day, 'Don't think I've forgotten what you did to me in Sister Mary Bertha's class.'"

"He had a memory like an elephant," Bobby Mack said. "And hold a grudge? Forever! We used to call him Fat Dahlgren in those days."

"Those days? Second grade?"

"Eight, nine years old, he must have weighed near 200 pounds," said Bobby Mack. "He was enormous! Used to get angry-- this vein would pop out on his forehead. And he had this odor about him. Used to call him Dahlgren Stink in those days... Jesus, Mary, and Joseph, those days!"

"That explains it," Hanratty said. "As long as I knew him he was always super conscious of his weight."

"Oh, yeah," Kalinyak said. "In high school, he slimmed down, took to running, worked out with weights."

"Became like a body builder," Bobby Mack said. "If he gained a pound he went crazy!"

"I'll say this much," Hanratty said. "I didn't know him the way yuns did. But he was smart. We got into an argument once about who was smarter. He insisted we do our multiplication tables! He beat me. Had to do 12 times 12 and I had no idea what it was and he just rattled it right off."

"Oh, yeah," Kalinyak said. "He was smart."

Bobby Mack nodded. "Like a cornered rat. He had what I like to call circular thought. He thought in circles. He could figure out what was happening in a situation from ten different angles and you'd still be working on the first angle."

"Lot of good it finally did him," Hanratty said.

"He knew how to make enemies, that's for sure." Bobby Mack said, "Chinese philosopher once said, if you don't feel it, go through the motions."

"Who said that?" said Hanratty.

"Some Chinese philosopher. I read it in a fortune cookie."

"I been doing that all my life," Kalinyak said.

"You have to keep doing it. One foot in front of the other. That's the way of a pro. When you were boxing, did you always feel it, did you always want to do it? You went through the motions and finally you felt it."

"You felt it, when that first punch hit you..."

"Well, yeah. But this is the way of the world. We're pros. This is our life."

"I want to feel again."

"Yuns guys is too deep," Hanratty said with a laugh.

"God bless you, Frank. If you feel it, you feel it. If not, one foot in front of the other. And one day it comes to an end."

"Great."

"Well, we know this. We just don't like to dwell on it."

"That's true. Let's not dwell on it."

"Good. Now let's see what we can do about Jack Dahlgren. He doesn't deserve it, but what the hell."

"I hear you. I got an uneasy feeling about this," said Kalinyak.

"How much do you know about the case?" Hanratty said.

"Nothing," Kalinyak said.

"Here's the broad outline: Dahlgren, in addition to being a sociopathic thief and creep, was also double-gaited, as they say in Texas."

"What?" Kalinyak said.

"He liked girls. And he liked boys. AC-DC."

"AC-DC. Doesn't surprise me," Kalinyak said. "But he didn't like girls. He hated girls."

"You gotta point there," Bobby Mack said.

"You know this is true. Even when we were kids..."

"True, true."

"There's a club down here, Aida, where the boys come to play," said Hanratty. "He would frequent this place. He had some freaky things he liked to do..."

"Okay."

Bobby Mack said, "He liked rough trade, tough guys. He would have them pick up a prostitute and they would have a threesome. Trouble was, sometime he would try to, shall we say, molest one of the others, sometimes the guy, sometimes the girl. Sometimes he would beat up the girl..."

"He served some time for this," Hanratty said.

"I had heard Jackie had served time. Didn't quite know what it was for."

"We kept getting complaints. He must have beat up a dozen or more whores over a period of time. The department would slap his hands," Hanratty said.

"Why'd they treat him like that?"

"He had a rabbi. Actually a couple of rabbis. Our good friend here was one—"

"He was an old, good friend of mine," Bobby said. "I would talk to him, and he would swear it was the last time and then he'd get some drinks in him—"

"Who was the other rabbi?" Kalinyak said.

"The Egg. Doyle Eggerman."

"Doyle? Why?"

"They were doing business together. You know Doyle'll do just about anything for a buck. And Doyle was his lawyer."

"Dahlgren's ex-wife works for him," Hanratty said.

Kalinyak raised his eyebrows and nodded. "Betty?" he said. "That's interesting."

"One hand washes the other," Bobby Mack said. "She's been working for the Egg since way back, when she and Dahlgren were first married even."

"Okay," said Hanratty, "so here's the broad outline: Jack's at the Aida, meets some hustler he knows. They're going to do a threesome, but the hustler insists Jack gets the girl. If there's going to be trouble, he doesn't want to be implicated too much. Jack's supposed to get back to him later that night. According to the hustler, he never does. Dahlgren ends up in some motel out on Route 19, dead. Now, he was seen with a hooker at the Hot Box Club over on Ninth Street, by the bridge—just down the road a ways. He left with her. Somehow they end up on Route 19, juke joint out there. They were seen dancing it up and hugging and all of that. They left. Checked into a motel nearby. Clerk saw him and her. Saw her leave a while later. Next morning maid goes into the room, he's cut wide, deep, and continuous."

"Hooker did it?"

"That's what it seems like, but there're all sorts of ramifications," Hanratty said.

"Come on back to the office," Bobby Mack said. "I'll show you what we have."

"You keep me out of this, hear?" Hanratty said. "Keep it at an arms length from me and the D.A. Do what you have to do, but any mess you make, Bobby Mack-- Greenfield Bob's-- going to have to clean it up."

Kalinyak laughed. "Greenfield Bob! That's what they called his father. 'Greenfield Bobby Mack...'"

"For years," Bobby Mack said, "I was Little Greenfield Bob. After my dad died over the years I've become just plain 'Greenfield Bobby Mack.'"

"What's this about St. Philomena's?" Kalinyak said.

Bobby Mack looked uncomfortable. "Nothing."

"Some people made some money on that," Hanratty said.

"Some people?" Kalinyak said.

"It's nothing. Forget it," Bobby Mack said. "Church in-fighting. The Pittsburgh Diocese and the Redemptorist Missionary order in New York who owned the land. A mess—"

"One hand washes the other," Hanratty said.

No one talked for a moment. "Doyle? Dahlgren?" Kalinyak said.

"Forget it," Bobby Mack said.

Bobby Mack and Kalinyak left Hanratty at Johnny McGuire's starting on his second liquid breakfast of the morning. They drove back to the D.A.'s offices in the Allegheny County Courthouse. It was Sunday, and Grant Street was practically empty. Bobby Mack parked at the curb. The great, dark, medieval, granite courthouse and jail loomed high above them.

They walked over to Forbes. Kalinyak referred to it as "Forbes Street," and Bobby Mack corrected him: it had become Forbes *Avenue*. "Town's been putting on some airs since you left," he said. "When we had mills, it was 'Forbes Street.' No more mills—Forbes Avenue."

Kalinyak looked up at the arching black stone link between the jail and the courthouse, known by the folk who worked here as "The Bridge of Sighs." "Them stones hold a lot of tears," said Bobby Mack. "Imagine all the weeping and gnashing of teeth as you're led across that."

Kalinyak indicated the courthouse. "They sentence them there?"

"And haul them off to the jail over that. 'Bridge of Sighs.'"

The offices were empty. Bobby Mack let himself in with an electronic card and found a cubicle at the rear. He opened a drawer and removed a file. He took a bottle of Glenlivet out of a desk drawer and poured himself a water glass full of scotch. "You sure you don't want—"

Kalinyak shook his head. "I'm very impressed," Bobby Mack said. He threw a pack of photographs onto the desktop in front of Kalinyak.

They showed a middle-aged man, nude, spread eagle on a narrow bed. There was blood all over the bed and the floor. The man was bound hands and feet to the bed with what looked like leather straps. There was a gag in his mouth. "Holy Jesus," Kalinyak said.

"Yeah," said Bobby Mack, lighting a Camel.

"He looked like he was in pretty good shape..."

"He took care of himself, worked out regularly at 24 Hour Fitness. Played racquetball. Competitive son of a bitch. He was always trying to get me on the court! 'Whatdya trying do, kill me?' I'd tell him. He and the Egg, Doyle Eggerman, played regularly."

"Jesus, look at that..." Kalinyak said holding a picture up close to his face.

"He was drunk, out like a light. She bound him to the bed and cut off his pecker and his balls. He bled to death. Look at this—" He passed Kalinyak another photograph. It was a quart-sized hourglass. "This is a four hour timer. If he woke up, he'd watch his life running out like sand. And this—"

He slid another photo to Kalinyak. It was a mirror over a sink. Scrawled in blood were the words, *"Baby, your out of time"*

"What does it mean?" Kalinyak said. Bobby Mack shook his head. "We're dealing with a nut here."

"I'd say so," Bobby Mack said. "Now the details of the killings, none of this has been released to the public, nothing about the castration, the hour glass, the blood note."

"So what do you think?"

"The first thought, of course, is that we have a crazed killer prostitute. But Jack Dahlgren had a lot of enemies. Maybe this is someone trying to make us think it's a prostitute."

"But the clerk said he came back there with a prostitute."

"That's right. But lookee here—he was known for these threesomes. He meets someone at the Aida, sets up a threesome. The hustler at the Aida gets together with the *whoor*, she brings him to the motel, he does the deed. I don't know. We've been questioning all the *whoors* and hustlers we can, and our old friend had dealings with a number of them. Some of the people admitted they didn't like him. Surprisingly, some were charmed by him. He could be very generous."

"He always was generous. Remember on his 16th birthday, he took us up to the Hill to get laid. He was paying..."

Bobby Mack began to laugh. "They pulled the Murphy game on us—"

"Pimp name of Long Gene," said Kalinyak.

"— pulled the okey-doke, conned Jackie out of every dollar. Was he angry! That vein in his forehead, how it used to bulge, you'd think it'd burst! He's yelling, 'We're the Huns! Rape and pillage! We're the Huns!'"

"So where are we?" Kalinyak said, spreading the photos in front of him.

"Like I said before, honest Injun, no one wants this thing solved. It's just you and me for old time sake."

"Where'd the killing take place?"

"Old motel out on Route 19. Remember Pine Valley?"

"The dance place?"

"Not far from there. That area has built up from our day. The whole place from the Pittsburgh line out to Zelienople is practically just city now."

"That used to be very rural."

"It's all built up, lot of juke joints out there. Motel row. And Pine Valley, the dance place, is still there."

"Lot of memories of that place."

"Lot of memories."

They both remained silent for a long time. "What does it mean?" Kalinyak said at last.

"What do you mean?"

"All of it. What does any of it mean?"

"His murder?"

"His murder. The whole thing. I'll tell you the truth, Bobby. Sometimes I just want to cash it all in..."

"Hey."

"I know. I'm not about to do that. But you start thinking and—Okay. Hourglass. Castrated. 'Baby your out of time" One thing's certain. Whoever wrote that, doesn't know their grammar..."

"What do you mean?"

"You're just dumb as she or he or it is—it should be y-o-u- apostrophe r-e. 'You are out of time,' not, 'your out of time.'"

"Great. So now all we have to look for is someone who's not too good with grammar. This is Hunky Town. You know what? If we have a population of a million in Greater Pittsburgh, we're talking about nine hundred thousand don't know shit about grammar. Ever hear of 'yuns?' This is the capital of 'yuns'!"

"What's the name of the fag club?"

"Aida."

"They open on Sundays?"

"Yeah. They're always open."

Kalinyak stood. "You guys pay for the car rental?"

"Hey, you got one from our pool. Here—" He reached in his desk and brought out a key. "The one out front, the one I was just using. And you might need this—" He passed a plastic ID card to Kalinyak. It read: "Allegheny County District Attorney, Special Investigator."

"Impressive."

"I printed that myself on my computer. It don't mean shit. If you fuck up, it's just me and you. We'll give you five bills a week plus expenses. How's that?"

"Good. Let me ask you: how bad do you want this to be solved?"

"My first impulse is to say I could give a fuck less. But you know, he was rotten to the core, but we all had something between us."

"We did."

"So for old time's sake. Let's get whoever did this." Bobby Mack suddenly became very serious. "I want to see the old fire," he said.

Frank Kalinyak shrugged. He shook his head. "No fire left, in me or the city. Remember the way it used to be, oh, when we were small kids? Then the industry died and all that iron began to rust. You could go along the rivers for miles, the Allegheny, the Monongahela, all the exploding, powerful mills pouring fire into the sky, the energy of the place: it was like going to an amusement park with all the light and energy, great plumes of fire, and now where is it? The Iron City Beer sign? What became of it?"

Bobby Mack shook his head. "No more," he said. "You know the difference between me and you? You're always thinking about this and that. And me? I just do. That's all I know. One foot in front of the other."

"In the old days, me too."

"I know this."

"Things changed."

"Yes," said Bobby Mack. "When your daughter—"

"Oh, yeah. It either turns you to religion or it turns you away from religion. That turned me away from everything."

"Well. That's what that does. But we're going to bring the old Frank Kalinyak back. The Hunky Hurricane!"

They left the courthouse building and Bobby Mack gave Kalinyak a tour of the renovated downtown area. "Over there, that building there, that's Mellon Bank Center,

Pittsburgh Plate Glass, U.S. Steel Building, 64 stories. These have all been built since you left town. The mills went down the crapper. But we built up with buildings. We got the corporations still here, U.S. Steel, Gulf, Koppers."

"I remember when the Clark Building was the be-all and end-all."

"We don't even talk about that no more. Though the candy bar sign is still up there." He pointed to a huge orange Clark sign in the shape of a candy bar atop the Clark Building.

He pointed across the Allegheny River. "They're going to be building a new baseball field and football field. Separate."

"Why separate?"

"Well, one'll be designed especially for football, another for baseball. This here bridge here, Sixth Street Bridge? They want to rename it for Roberto Clemente."

"That's nice."

"Oh, sure."

Bobby Mack left Kalinyak at this hotel. "I'll pick you up about seven for that thing at Eggerman's."

"What do you wear, a suit or what?"

"It's going to be just the Mirror Street guys. You could come in a jock-strap, no one would say anything."

"What about Magoczy?"

"Called him this morning, told him you were in town. He said to say, hello. No, he won't be there."

"Strange duck, Magoczy."

"Always was. The Magpie! You know when we were kids I always thought he might be a little light in the loafers…"

"That's interesting. Why would you say that?"

"Well, you know we were out looking to get laid. He was very reticent in that area."

"He was shy."

"I know. I think the church is a good thing for him."

"As I remember, we had something with him, where we got him laid…"

"He never went through with it."

"Was that it?"

"Gang bang," Bobby Mack said.

"I remember. Some girl Jack Dahlgren got for all of us."

"As best I remember."

"I don't remember too well." He felt a stir of uneasiness, pain, guilt. "I'll bet Magpie remembers, though. Damn, he had a memory."

"I'll pick you up a little before seven. You need the car, it'll be parked over on Ross Street, by the Bridge of Sighs."

In the room, surrounded by the pictures of his dead daughter, Kalinyak felt restless and sad and lost. Who did he have left in the world that he was close to? His old sandlot football team, The Mirror Street Aces? Their Horsemen of the Apocalypse, the Huns—with Dahlgren now dead, there were four: himself, Magoczy, Bobby Mack, Doyle Eggerman? All strangers to him really.

No wife, parents dead, relatives, those he knew, most of them dead, also. A married sister living in Alaska—hadn't spoken to her in years. At the death of his father fifteen years ago—his mother had died when they were very young—he and his sister had had differences over what to do with the house on Mirror Street. He wanted to keep it in the family. His daughter was alive then, five years old. He had an idea—it was embarrassingly silly to him now— of retiring to Greenfield some day. His daughter would take care of him when he was old.

It turned out he had no say in the matter. His father had left the house to his sister. She sold it.

He didn't even come back home for the funeral.

His father, a mill worker, had been a tough, miserable old guy, particularly after the death of Kalinyak's mother. A morose man, a heavy drinker, he exuded contempt for Kalinyak, and Kalinyak couldn't wait to leave home as soon as possible after graduation from high school.

He changed out of the second suit he had brought, a light seersucker thing, and put on slacks and a tee shirt, tennis shoes.

The Aida Lounge was three blocks from the hotel, not far from the old Stanley movie theater, now the Benedict Center for the Performing Arts. It was long and dark and narrow.

The velvet walls were covered with posters and photos of Sophia Loren in a filmed version of Verdi's opera "Aida."

It was Sunday afternoon and the lounge was quiet. There was a long, silver metal bar and silver metal tables. A smoky mirror ran the length of the bar. The bartender wore a dark brown sleeveless shirt, a thick leather belt with a large silver buckle. Four wispy young men sat at the bar. Several more well-built, muscular men lounged at tables against the wall.

Kalinyak sat at the bar and ordered an Iron City beer. A small, lithe man, lean and muscular, with a shaved head and moustach sat next to him. He looked like a boxer, lightweight or welterweight. Behind lightly tinted glasses, he had dark, dead eyes. "Where you from?" the man asked. He had a surprisingly heavy voice.

"Out of town."

"Where?"

"Arizona. Tucson."

"I've never been. Never been out of Pennsylvania. I'm from Oil City. My name's Cory." He waited for Kalinyak's name, which didn't come. "What're you looking for?"

"Information."

"Ah. Cop?"

"Not exactly."

"What does that mean?"

"Private investigator."

"Okay. You here about that guy who was murdered."

"Why do you say that?"

Cory laughed softly. "He was killed more than a month ago. Cops have been here every day, practically. I'm a regular here, so I been talking to them almost every day."

"What'd they want to know?"

"Did I know dude that was killed?"

"Did you?"

"I knew him. Freaky fuck."

"In what way?"

"Look, this is a fag joint and you no doubt think I'm a queer. I'm not. But I am a predator. I do make bucks off queers."

"And this guy who was killed, he was what?"

"You know, he was freaky. He wanted me to get a girl and go at it with her while he watched."

"Did you get him a girl?"

"I told him I knew this freak, hung around over at the Hot Box. If he wanted to talk to her, set something up, I'd play ball. I had the feeling he wanted to get this girl and rape her and beat her up. He was a nut case, hated women. He told me some stories what he had done with them. And his eyes would always light up."

"Did he meet the girl?"

"I don't know."

"Cops said he did."

"Then he did. I don't know. I told him, look, here's the girl's name, what she looks like. You can find her most every evening at the Hot Box. She's a pro. It's gonna cost you. Fine, he says. I tell him, when and where you want the scene you call me on my cell phone. He never called."

"Who was this girl, the pro?"

"Name's Marika. German girl."

"Where does she live?"

"Don't know. She just hangs at the Hot Box. Fucks for money, has scenes for money. Freak. I think she spent time in a nut house."

"Why do you say that?"

"Just a sense I had of her. Why're you asking so many questions?"

"I'm interested in the guy who was murdered."

"Why?"

"Old friend."

"Ah. For a guy who was a real freak, he was not a bad guy. I think he was misunderstood."

"In what way?"

"Well, you take a guy who seems to be a regular guy in every way and then he finds out he likes dick. He likes pussy, but the also likes dick. That would be very unsettling, would cause dude to behave in a tense way. What did you say your name was?"

"I didn't." Kalinyak paused, set Cory with a hard cop look. "Frank."

"Nice meeting you, Frank."

"He wouldn't have mentioned me. I hadn't seen him in a long time. Where's the Hot Box?"

"Over on Ninth, just by the Frick Hotel."

"I'd like to see this Marika."

"I can take you there. It's within walking distance."

"How much?"

"It's not like that."

"Come on—"

"One of these days I'll bill you."

"She'd be there at this hour? Sunday afternoon?"

"These people are very unreliable. But she definitely is a money making machine. She'd work all night, all day if she could."

They left the Aida and walked to the Hot Box Club. The day was hot and muggy. Kalinyak and Cory were perspiring. "I'm praying for rain again," Cory said. "Can't stand this humidity. No, your friend was conflicted. He would sometimes tell me things."

"Such as?"

"He had had more homosexual flings than the other way around."

"He was a homosexual?" Kalinyak said.

"He had an identity crisis. You and me, we have normal desires. When you get someone with fag inclinations, you got someone who's conflicted."

Kalinyak found the black deadness in Cory's eyes unsettling. This guy's nuts, he was thinking: amazing how I can come into an environment, even one wall-to-wall with people, bar, disco, party— if there's one psycho in the crowd, he or she will gravitate to me. When he was younger it troubled him. What was it in him that attracted the sickos? Later, in his police work, he realized it was an asset.

Suddenly his daughter rose up in his mind, so clear he thought he could kiss her image. Again! Again! She was with him always. Dear God! He'd meet someone and his mind would start going over and over things. Is the murderer of his daughter thin like this person? Does he have the same dead eyes? Could this person possibly be her killer?

It was ridiculous, of course. They were almost a continent away from Tucson; years had gone by. But, still, his mind was racing, dread in the pit of his stomach, his hands damp with perspiration.

Is this creep him? Is this who killed my daughter?

He closed his eyes, waved his hand in front of him, as if to banish thoughts of her. "What?" Cory said.

"Nothing. Nothing."

The Hot Box was a narrow storefront in a row of battered clapboard buildings not far from the river. The street that it was on was on the edge of the downtown area. There was a bar on the corner, "Charlie Adam's Ringside Café."

In the old days, you would have followed the street uphill for less than a block and you'd be in the Hill District, the city's black area. Most of the Hill had been torn down to make way for the Civic Arena.

The windows and door of The Hot Box were painted black. There was a poster advertising a stripper who danced with giant peacock feathers. Kalinyak and Cory entered. An air-conditioner hummed weakly, pumping out moist, warm air. There were two gaudily dressed women in their forties sitting with an older man at a back table. There were several middle-age men in work clothes at the bar.

The bartender was a large black man who looked as though he had once played football.

"Hey, Preacher..." Cory said as they approached the bar. The bartender, who was occupied washing glasses, didn't acknowledge him. "Has my friend been around?"

"Who's that?" the bartender said without looking up.

"That German girl. You know the German girl I come in with every once in a while."

"German girl?"

"Marika. Sexy thing. Blonde. Bright blue eyes."

"Oh, yeah. Naw, she hasn't been around. Cops have been asking about her. What can I fix you?"

Kalinyak had had enough of voluble, grating Cory. "I gotta run," he said.

"Where're you rushing?" Cory said.

Kalinyak consulted his wristwatch. "I have obligations today."

"She could come around."

"Not if the cops are asking about her," Kalinyak said. He put two twenties down on the bar. "Give my friend what he wants," he said to the bartender.

"No problem."

"And if Marika shows, give me a call. You're Preacher?"

"That's right."

"What do you preach?"

"Minding my own business."

"Here's my cell phone number. If you mind some other person's business, it could be a few bucks." He wrote his number down on a cocktail napkin and passed it to the bartender. He wrote the number down for Cory, also. "And if you can't reach me on the cell, try this—"

"What's this?"

"D.A.'s office. Ask for Bobby Mack..." He attempted to slip him a ten, but Cory pushed his hand away. "Naw, naw. I'd like to help. That guy didn't seem to be such a bad guy."

"Well, you're not right on that, but that's okay."

Chapter
Three

Bobby Mack steered his Lincoln Town Car through the winding streets North of Forbes, beneath immense trees: linden, maple, and larch. Screened by the trees, angles of the great mansions that dominated the area flashed by, massive stone, brick, and marble edifices that had once belonged to Pittsburgh's captains of industry. "That's the old Carnegie place there," Bobby Mack pointed out to Kalinyak. "Frick over there. That used to be George Westinghouse's spread..."

Theresa McGinness was not with Bobby Mack this night. "Once a week is all I can put up with her," he explained to Kalinyak. "She likes to get laid. To me, it's like taking a warm piss. One day a week I give her."

He turned on Wilkens, then onto Woodbine Road. Bobby Mack, in a suit of wash-and-wear seersucker, was in an expansive mood. "I love this boat," he said, snaking the Town Car down the narrow road "Jack Nicklaus Signature

Series. Onyx exterior, cream-colored leather seats, krypton tint headlights and windows, Dayton wheels."

"Rides nice," Kalinyak said.

"Look up there," Bobby Mack said. "The very top." A huge stone and brick Tudor house, barely visible through stands of beech and oak soaring into the night sky, dominated a hill above the road. The cobblestone road up to the house was flanked by carriage lights. "Used to belong to that oil guy, Benedict."

"Fucking Eggerman," Kalinyak said. "Had to do well."

"Doing better than well. Used to drive Dahlgren crazy, envious fuck that he was."

He pulled the Town Car onto a circular parking area of red brick in front of the house. A white Rolls Corniche, a Mercedes, and a Jag were directly in front of the house, as well as a half dozen lesser cars. Bobby Mack parked next to the Jag, and he and Kalinyak climbed the stone stairs to the great oak front door.

A pert, gray-haired woman in a black-and-white uniform admitted them to the house. She led them through a marble entryway into a massive living room, paneled in oak, with thick oaken ceiling beams. One wall was covered with books. Nursing cocktails, looking awkward and uncomfortable, were the Mirror Street Aces and their wives. A large red-jacketed man with black waistcoat moved through the group, offering drinks and canapés. Through a side door, Kalinyak could see others of the Aces and their wives on a lighted patio. "The Huns are here!" Buddha Kruisper, in his canary yellow sport jacket, called out. "Rape and pillage! Rape and pillage..." He hugged Kalinyak hard.

"I give," said Kalinyak, laughing. Buddha pounded him on the arm and they both laughed.

Doyle Eggerman approached. Behind him was his wife and another woman, an attractive redhead. She had a small smile on her face. "Betty Malloy," Kalinyak said.

"How did you know?" Betty Malloy said. Her smile widened. It was dazzling.

"You haven't changed."

"Since I was, what, seventeen? Last time I saw you?"

"Younger. I was going up to Clarion. You must have been thirteen, fourteen," said Kalinyak.

"How've you been?"

"Not too bad. You look nice. You've grown up."

"Thank you. You look good. Distinguished."

"Which means old."

"No. Distinguished is distinguished. You've been—all right?"

"Not too bad."

"I heard about what happened," she said. He didn't answer. "I'm very sorry. It must have been—" He shrugged. "I can't imagine it."

"Well. How've you been?"

"Okay. Working with Doyle."

"The brains of the operation," Doyle said, hugging Betty and laughing.

"She was always very smart," Kalinyak said.

"Doyle couldn't exist without her," Kari said. "And before that, Dahlgren. She ran his whole operation."

"No one told Dahlgren what to do," Betty said.

"You got that right," Doyle said.

"For a hunky from Mirror Street, Egg, you've done well," Kalinyak said, gazing round at the paneled walls, the marble fireplace, the large, cut-glass chandelier.

"For a hunky from Mirror Street," Doyle said.

"Smartest hunky in Greenfield," Kari Eggerman said.

"Look how hard it is for her," Doyle said. "Saying the word..."

"Hunky, hunky, hunky," Kari said.

Bobby Mack had extricated himself from Buddha and joined them. "Who's the smartest hunky in Greenfield?" Bobby said.

"Doyle," Betty Molloy said.

"Naw," Bobby Mack said. "Jack Dahlgren was smarter."

"He wasn't a hunky, strictly speaking," Doyle said.

"Okay, he was a mick. But he was a hunky mick. Micks, guineas, polacks. Anyone from Mirror Street to Greenfield Avenue is a hunky..."

"That's what I believe," Kari said.

"The question," Kalinyak said "is, how Doyle landed you?"

"He's very sneaky," she said. "You thought Jack Dahlgren was sneaky?"

"She was out of touch," Doyle said, indicating his wife.

"I was North of Forbes."

"You were the epitome," Kalinyak said.

"I was the epitome," Kari said, nodding her head. "We had Coburn's chem, qualitative analysis together, Doyle and I. This is one smart guy, I thought. Then when he beat Oldendick out for class president— he made that speech..."

"Rising tide lifts all boats," Kalinyak said.

"That's right!" Betty Malloy said. "How did you remember that?"

"I was thinking, damn, the Egg is smart. What does any of this have to do with tides and boats?"

"Jack Dahlgren was vice-president," Bobby Mack said.

"Vice is right," Kari said.

"Don't speak ill of, you know," Bobby Mack said, glancing over at Betty.

"Speak ill all you want," Betty said. "When I heard about, you know, the killing? I didn't feel a thing. I didn't shed one tear. I'm sorry, but that's just the way it is."

"Where're the kids?" Bobby Mack said to Kari.

"Trisha's up in Boston—"

"Good town, Boston," Bobby said.

"Boston University, going for her masters degree."

"The boys?" Bobby said. "Football?"

"Golf," Kari said.

"At Miami U," Doyle said, "majoring in girls on the beach."

"Lucky they got a rich dad," Bobby Mack said.

"Your daughter?" Kari said. "Jenny? Pretty girl."

Bobby Mack shook his head. He reached over and took a glass of champagne from the server's tray as he moved past them. He waved the glass at the group, then downed the champagne. "Makes me sick to my stomach! Took after her mother in the respect of, well, you know, substance abuse. Used to come home when she was a teen-ager, she and the old lady'd be sloshed in front of the television set, watching soap operas. One day I just lost it, kicked the damn screen in, 'Your life is a fucking soap opera!' Picked up the set, smashed it against the wall, walked out and never came back. Now she won't have anything to do with me. Been in and out of the jackpot, drugs, prostitution, kiting checks, you name it."

"The mother was—?" Kalinyak said.

"Molly Worshack."

"Oh, yeah," Kalinyak said. "From Saline Street."

"Biggest tits in Greenfield," Doyle said.

"Oh, yeah. You married her?" Kalinyak said.

"Stupidest thing I ever did in my life," Bobby Mack said.

"Where is she now?"

"She's around. Who knows what she's doing? Working hard to kill herself, no doubt. Some people'd called it a mercy killing. Good riddance."

"You don't mean that," Betty said.

"Naw, you're right. I don't. It's just she caused so much heartache with me and the kid. Hey!" He flagged down the server and grabbed another glass of champagne. "This guy here," he said, indicating Kalinyak. "Would you believe it? Off the sauce."

"That's good," Betty said. "Let's talk, you and me..."

Doyle Eggerman laughed. "Oh, look at that!"

"Well, you told me," Kari said.

"What?" Doyle said.

"They were good friends in high school," Bobby Mack said.

"Yes, we were," Betty said. "I always liked Frank. There was something genuine about him, honest."

"I liked you, too," Kalinyak said, trying to make a joke of it, but it came out forced.

"This is cute," Kari said.

Kalinyak and Betty Malloy walked out onto the patio. Behind a portable bar was the fellow in the red jacket and waistcoat. "What do you want to drink?" Kalinyak asked.

"White wine."

Kalinyak ordered a ginger ale. "What's this?" Betty said. "You used to be a drinker."

"No more. I give it up. Got me into a lot of trouble."

"You're better off," she said. "I always thought a lot of Dahlgren's problems came from the sauce."

"He would have had problems if he only drank milk..."

She laughed. "You're right on that."

They walked beyond the patio along a flagstone path. Immense larch and oak trees lined the path. The air was damp, heavy and fragrant with verbena. Cicadas thrummed about them. "You have no idea how stupid I feel about that," Betty said. "No one would have ever thought of me with Jack Dahlgren. Me most of all!"

"Boggles the mind."

"Life is like a wildcat that leaps up into your face! You do something and you don't know why! That was my life with Dahlgren. Wham!"

"I mean I knew you were married to him. He was the father of your kids. And it—"

"Boggled your mind."

"It did."

She grew quiet. She seemed suddenly uncomfortable and Kalinyak regretted having come down so hard on Dahlgren with her. "What are you doing here, Frank?" she said after a while. "I know you—you didn't just come for the reunion—"

"Bobby Mack wants to find out who killed Jack. For Auld Lang Syne, he says."

"Ah! Sherlock Holmes..."

"To be honest? On a gut level? I don't give a damn about who killed Dahlgren."

"Understandable," Betty Malloy said. "I heard you had become a cop."

"Was. Retired now." They stood in silence for a long moment. "Yeah. When I heard you had married Jack—"

"You were taken aback," she said with a faint touch of irony. She smiled a quiet smile and Kalinyak was thinking, what a good, fine lady this is. He knew why he had liked her so much when they were kids. There was a shy, sweet, intelligent quality to her; a good person, a person of quality.

"Jack Dahlgren was ambitious," Betty said. "For a Greenfield boy, we liked that. And I guess I was gullible, stupid, and a little crazy. I thought I could— handle him, change him. I was so—silly. And what became of you? You were at Clarion a short while, then you went into the army. And then I would hear a few things from time to time."

"I felt if I stayed around here—what would I have become? Jack would have got me hustling vinyl siding with him. When we were in high school even that was his game."

Betty laughed. "The old 'do you have the fifties?' scam..."

"You remember? "

"Excuse me, ma'am, did the man with the fififties come by?'" she said, imitating a siding salesman.

Damn, she's cute, Kalinyak thought. "Good. Very good." He went into the follow up: " 'We put up the siding for you, free for nothing, nothing for free! Every house in this area that buys, you get fifty dollars!' " They both laughed. "Jack'd have those fifty dollar bills hanging out of every pocket. He could sure work that scam. Even in high school! Who knows? Maybe that's what I should have become, siding salesman..."

"You don't have to make excuses for your life."

"No, I feel I do. I feel I've messed my life up."

"Why do you say that?"

"I had a marriage that— married the wrong person."

"What else is new?" Betty took his hand. "You were always the best. As they used to say in the neighborhood, you were real good people. The tragedy with your little girl—you never deserved that."

"And you," Kalinyak said. "Jack Dahlgren. What was that like?"

"He was a psychopath. Of course, naïve girl that I was, church-going Catholic kid, what did I know about psychopaths? We had children, amazingly they're doing very well. Like Doyle's kids, they're away at college, Penn State both of them. They both play football, too, like you and Jack. Greenfield kids."

"Penn State? We had to settle for Clarion State Teachers."

"They're good. And they're smart. They'll be in business. They're going to do all right."

"How did his, you know, his getting killed affect them?"

"Neither of them liked him very much. They felt he deserved something like that. I think we all knew he would come to a bad end. You've heard about his sexual, what should we call it, deviations?"

"I would have never thought—"

"Who would have? Was there anyone who lusted after women more than Jack?"

"True. He loved them and he hated them."

"Yes, he did. He wanted to humiliate them."

"What was that like?"

"There was a time early in the marriage when I felt he was trying to drag me into whatever weirdness he had going on. I told him that if he wanted to stay married he must never bring that sort of thing into the marriage. We had a strange relationship. He was bright, he was exciting, he was fun. He treated me very well. I'm the only person in the world, I think, who he treated well. He put me on a pedestal, and he kept me there."

"I see."

"He despised women, and yet— Well, you knew his mother..."

"Junie? She was tough."

"A monster."

"Yes, I suppose she was. His father was no bed of roses."

"Rotten, that's true. Alcoholic. Thug. Well, you remember him."

"I remember Jack knocking him down a flight of stairs," Kalinyak said. "We were kids, fourteen, fifteen, laying around Junie's bedroom. She was in her slip. We were all drinking, I don't know, rotgut, Thunderbird wine or something. Albert came home from the mill, LTV Coke Works in Hazelwood, drunker'n anything, starts cursing her, calling her a whore, whatever, and she gave back as good as she was getting. Albert clipped her with the back of his hand and

Jack lifted him up and dragged him to the top of the staircase and threw him down, hard. Broke his nose bouncing down the stairs. Blood everywhere. Fun and games in the Dahlgren household."

"What are your plans?" Betty said. He shook his head. "You going to stay for a while?"

"Yeah. For Bobby Mack."

"Auld Lang Syne..."

"Yep."

"Jack's funeral was pathetic. I don't think a half dozen people showed up. And they were there to celebrate..."

"Sad, I guess."

"Humiliating."

"I can imagine. He was in siding. What else—?"

"He was in everything, including some drug dealings."

"Really?"

"Began with the siding, did very well with that, hanging tin. Then he started a series of community papers. He would do a paper for instance, for the blacks, The Hill District Gazette, throw away. Go to companies around town, solicit advertising. 'You took out a five hundred dollar ad last year. Shall we go 750 this year? You know there's been a lot of unrest in your area. You don't want to give the blacks any excuse to be angry with you...' Something like that. For the longest time, I thought he really wanted to do something for these communities. Then I found out, he would print up just enough copies to send to the company with their ad."

"Scam."

"Oh, yeah. Well, you know, that was Jack, his middle name. What was worse—I only learned this after we had gone our separate ways—was that he took to distributing narcotics, different stuff, and to stretch the supply, he'd have his people step on it with other substances. He never knew what his crew would throw in there. People occasionally died. No, he was a very bad person."

"And you stayed with him—"

"Fifteen years." She shook her head. "I was so naïve. I just never knew what was going on. That's the way all the neighborhood girls were." She shrugged, hugged her arms around herself, and gazed out at the trees.

"You look very good," Kalinyak said.

"You look good, too."

"Can you imagine if you and I had—"

"Through the years I would think about it," Betty said.

"Really?"

"I'd think about you. How good and honest you were. You would have made a good husband."

"No. I was too self-absorbed, too committed to being a cop. A real cop. Incorruptible. I wanted to rid the earth of all the bad people. After my daughter—well, I went a little nuts."

"Of course. Who wouldn't?"

"You know what we ought to do? Drive out to Pine Valley some evening. For old time's sake."

"It's still there."

"I heard."

"Jack was killed out there. By the dance place."

"Bobby Mack told me."

Betty drained her wine glass, stared at the bottom; held it up and looked at Kalinyak through it. She laughed and put the glass down.

"It's good seeing you, kid."

"It's good seeing you, too, Frank."

She leaned forward and they hugged. He gave her a small peck on the cheek and they walked back toward the house. "You were always like a little sister to me," Kalinyak said.

"I always felt the Mirror Street Aces were my big brothers, Buddha and Gus Magoczy and you and everyone."

The group was in the dining room, lined up to eat. Several men in red coats served the food buffet style from a large table along one wall, roast beef, steak, several pastas and salads. "Whatever became of Sarah Jo Kaczmarek?" Tino Bronk said.

"What brought that up?" Bobby Mack said.

"We were talking about the time we played the Tartars and Sarah Jo was there with, who was it, Jimmy Flynn? And Dahlgren threw a fit, wanted to fight Jimmy."

"Were they going together?" Tino's wife, Kitty, said.

"Everybody went with her," Don Smith said.

"Come on now," Betty said. "She was very sweet. And very pretty."

"She went bad, as I remember," Doyle Eggerman said. "Didn't she become a prostitute, or something?"

"She did go very bad," Bobby Mack said.

"She was a beautiful girl," Kalinyak said. "Dahlgren messed her up."

"That's right," Bobby said. "I remember that now."

"What?" said Betty.

"Oh, Dahlgren was screwing her—this was before he met you. Junior year. She was in love with him. Who knows what went on..."

"Didn't she kill herself?" Doyle Eggerman said. "I seem to remember something. Or she overdosed. Came to a bad end, that I'm sure of."

Kalinyak grew very quiet. He felt a terrible weight descend on him, the weight of the past, the weight of Jack Dahlgren. "I think Magoczy was right," he said. "Jack was the devil."

"He was a Hun," Buddha Kruisper said. "No more, no less. Long live the Aces, long live the Huns!"

They all drank to that. They told stories of the old days. They re-played the Tartar-Mirror Street Aces games. They drank beer and wine and champagne and whiskey. They sang songs, Kalinyak and Bobby Mack and Buddha and Tino Bronk harmonizing as they used to do on the corner of Mirror Street and Kennebec or in front of Reese's Pool Hall on Greenfield Avenue. They talked about the boys and girls they grew up with. Tino Bronk's wife, Kitty, brought up Sarah Jo Kaczmarek again. "I can't get it out of my head," she said drunkenly. "There was something between her and Dahlgren—"

"She liked Dahlgren," Betty Malloy said. "They all liked Dahlgren."

Everyone laughed. "But no one ever went bad like Sarah Jo. Not like that," said Kitty Bronk

"She was a real religious girl," Buddha Kruisper said.

"Yes, she was," said the Egg.

"What happened there?" Donny Smith said. "I knew her from St. Philomena's way back. We were little kids over there. She was almost like a nun."

"She ran into Dahlgren," Buddha said.

"Let's get off this subject," Bobby Mack said. "It happens to people. People go bad. Happened in my own family..."

"I remember her being very beautiful," Betty Malloy said. "So beautiful. And so sweet-looking."

"Life does things," Buddha said.

Kalinyak had grown somber. "St. Philomena's. I can't believe it. No more," he said.

"It's the world," Bobby Mack said. "One day she's St. Philomena's, one day not so much a saint. What can you do?"

"The fun we had! Baseball. Father Stan," Kalinyak said. "The mine shaft..."

"Oh, yeah," said Buddha Kruisper. "We did some exploring down there."

"There was a period there when Jack Dahlgren was breaking into houses," Don Smith said.

"Dahlgren! Naw..." said Buddha.

"Used to hide his swag in the mine shaft."

"Also the pond in front." Kalinyak shook his head. "St. Philomena's..."

"Gone," Betty said. "No more."

"That's—that's just shocking..."

"Nothing shocks me these days," Kari Eggerman said.

"The bottom line," Buddha said. "Life, you know."

"Inevitable," Bobby Mack said.

"But how did it happen?" Kalinyak said.

"The Pittsburgh Diocese," Betty Malloy said. "They dumped her. Sold off the church, the land."

"I just can't fathom it. I'm stunned..."

"These things happen," said Doyle Eggerman.

"Someone made a bundle there..." Kalinyak said. Doyle shrugged. "The church was a gem. You had all that land. Your own coal mine, even..."

"It was complicated," said Doyle.

"It was," said Bobby Mack.

"Once she was more or less desanctified they washed their hands, the Diocese," said Kitty Bronk.

"Oh, sure," said Bobby Mack.

"A Catholic missionary society in Brooklyn owned the land," Kitty said.

"The Redemptorists," said Doyle, staring out the window into the night, abstracted.

Betty Malloy said, "St. Philomena's was the only church in the diocese that wasn't owned by the bishops."

"That was it. That was the bare fact," said Bobby Mack. "Nothing anybody could do."

Everyone grew quiet. "What are you doing here, Frank?" Eggerman said finally.

"You invited me."

"No, I mean what brought you to the reunion?"

"I brought him," Bobby Mack said.

Doyle Eggerman smiled. It was a quiet, self-satisfied smile. "Frankie Kalin, the Kalinyak, can do something the police can't?" There was a vaguely nasty edge in his voice.

"It's not that," Kalinyak said. "As I've been told, no one's interested in finding out who killed Jack."

"You got that right."

"And I'll be honest with you, I don't give a care either."

"I'll ask again: why are you here?" Doyle said.

Kalinyak did not speak. "Because that's the kind of guy Kalin is," Bobby Mack said. "He doesn't like it that one of our own guys was killed. Auld Lang Syne, as we say."

Doyle nodded and broke into a wide grin. "I know, Kalin. I'm just messing with you. Let's have another drink!"

As the evening ended, Kalinyak walked with Betty Malloy out to her car. He turned her to him and kissed her. She had a small smile on her face. "I'm sorry," he said. "I just— wanted to—"

"I'm glad you did. We'll drive out to Pine Valley. Maybe later in the week."

"That'll be good," he said.

Chapter Four

It was almost one a.m. when Bobby Mack dropped Kalinyak at the hotel. Bobby was drunk, but he barely showed it. He had always been able to hold his liquor. Iron City Iron Man, they used to call him in addition to Little Greenfield Bobby Mack. He was driving over to see Theresa McGinness. "She gets lonely," he said, by way of explanation. "It's not only the sex thing. She likes me as a human being."

"How did you meet her?"

"We prosecuted her husband. He was a jacker. Dufus! Grabbed a truck off Thorne Run Road, Moon Township, nickel and dime stuff. Went away for a long time, left her with bills, no way to survive. I felt bad for her."

"You did a good thing."

"What difference does it make? Do you think anyone cares? Do you think she cares? Not really..."

With some effort, Kalinyak got out of the car. "Damn," he said. His right leg had stiffened up on him. "Munhall game," he said.

"Billy Hayes, opening kick-off. Chop block," Bobby Mack said.

"Damn," Kalinyak said, massaging his leg just above the knee. "How do you remember that?"

Bobby Mack shrugged. "Well. You know what this life is," he said.

"Oh, sure."

"We're born," Bobby Mack said, "we have troubles. Then we die."

"That makes me feel real good," Kalinyak said.

"My philosophy," Bobby Mack said. He saluted with two fingers and drove off.

Kalinyak stretched his leg, tested it, then limped toward the hotel's revolving door. As he crossed the hotel lobby, his cell phone rang. It was Preacher, the bartender at the Hot Box Club. "That German girl's here, the one you asked about."

"I'll be right there."

He hurried back out on Smithfield Street. The cabstand was empty, the block deserted. He crossed Smithfield and moved at an awkward run down Fifth Avenue to Liberty. He turned onto Ninth Street.

The Hot Box was empty except for Preacher, who was tidying up, washing glasses, drying them haphazardly and setting them on a towel behind the bar. "She just left," he said.

"Damn," Kalinyak said.

"Antsy. She just run. May have seen me on the phone."

Back outside, Kalinyak looked desperately up and down the block. Someone was almost at the river, moving swiftly away. He ran full out toward the person, a blonde woman in a long leather coat, going at a half-run toward the Ninth Street Bridge. At the foot of the bridge, Kalinyak caught up with her. "Hey, hey!"

She turned. A woman in her late twenties, she was beautiful in a hard way. Her eyes were very blue and cold as shards of ice. Her face was taut. "Who are you?" She had a quiet voice, a slight accent. She was wearing a thick, sweet perfume, heavy, overpowering in its cheapness. Underneath her leather coat she wore a cotton dress. Her hair was piled in a tall bouffant.

"I want to talk to you..."

"Do I know you?"

"I was a friend of the man who was killed..."

"I don't know any man who was killed."

"I had heard that you were with him on the evening..."

"You have me confused with someone else."

"You're a professional?"

She studied Kalinyak and her gaze was cold and hard, marble eyes, Kalinyak was thinking. "You're a cop, no?" she said.

"No."

Her hands were in her leather coat. She brought the right one out. It held a Heckler & Koch Nine Millimeter Automatic. "Just walk with me," she said quietly. "Don't do anything, nothing. Don't be stupid or I'll kill you."

She motioned him toward the bridge.

"What do you want?" Kalinyak said, outwardly calm. Fear was on his heart, a hand of ice gripping it, squeezing it.

She indicated that he walk across the bridge. "I have my car on the other side," she said.

"Where are we going?" Kalinyak said.

"To have some fun..."

There was a frozen, mechanical-doll quality about her, and the fear in Kalinyak was so deep that it almost paralyzed him. He said to himself, she's going to kill me. "What is this? What's it about?"

"You don't know?"

"No."

"I think you do."

She was a step behind him. The odor of her perfume was like a knife in his brain. He glanced back. He could see, under her marble exterior, a gleam of excitement in her eyes, and that caused him to feel even greater fear.

A large truck sped along Ninth Street and up onto the bridge. "Just keep walking," she said. As the truck neared them, he could sense that she was distracted, and Kalinyak made his move. He grabbed her gun arm and dove to one side, flinging her toward the street. The gun went off. The bullet hit the bridge railing with a whine. The truck swerved, and Kalinyak ripped the gun from her. She bit his hand and the gun fell. She dove for it, but he kicked at it, and it slid across the walkway and under the railing and disappeared into the water below.

The truck driver, a large man in a dark sweatshirt, was out of his truck, a tire iron in one hand. The German girl ran across the bridge for the north side of the river. Kalinyak started after her and the truck driver hit him across the back with the tire iron. Kalinyak felt the air rush from him and intense pain across his shoulders. "I'm a cop!" he yelled. He had pulled the plastic ID card Bobby Mack had prepared for him: "Allegheny County District Attorney, Special Investigator."

The truck driver looked warily at him. He reached out and took the ID and studied it. "I thought it was a mugging or something," he said.

"Drive across the bridge."

The driver climbed up into the truck cab and Kalinyak got into the passenger side. It was a yeast truck, Federal Yeast. The driver's name on his sweatshirt was "Casey." The interior of the truck smelled rancid. "Got to get this stuff out to the bakeries early," Casey said. At the far end of the bridge there was a parking area. They drove down the length of the lot. There were a half-dozen cars scattered about. Kalinyak got out and investigated each car. They were all locked.

"I can't wait," Casey said.

Kalinyak straightened up and rotated his head. "You damn near broke my back."

"You shoulda wore a uniform. Here for your troubles..." He threw Kalinyak a loaf of foul-smelling Federal Yeast wrapped in wax paper, then drove off.

Kalinyak walked back across the bridge. He paused at where he and the girl had scuffled. He gazed down into the black water of the river. He noted where the gun had fallen. He marked the spot with a chunk of the yeast and threw the rest into the water.

The door at the Hot Box Club was locked; he banged on it, and Preacher let him in. "She come in about an hour or so before you showed," he said, sipping at a cup of black coffee. "Said she was waiting for that fellow, what's his name, was in here with you?"

"Cory?"

"Said she was waiting for this Cory. I figured maybe you was meeting both of them. Then I decided to call you."

"Cory show?"

"She called someone, then took off. Hey, damn, hard work, *talking, telling tales*, know what I mean? My mouth here getting fatigued..." Kalinyak passed him a twenty-dollar bill, reminding himself to submit an expense chit to Bobby Mack. "Uh huh, that make it better," Preacher said. "Yeah, that good."

Someone was tapping on the front door glass, a blonde, gaudily dressed, with thick make-up. She had two friends with her, similarly attired. Preacher opened the door a crack. "Hey, skank-os," Preacher said, "closing time."

"Who you calling a skank, jigger?" a short, dark-haired Spanish-looking girl said.

"If the foo shits," Preacher said.

"It's only five to," the dark-haired girl said.

The bartender shrugged. "What can I do you?" Preacher said.

"Straight shots, whiskey," the blonde said. She was tall and quite attractive. "Doubles." She wagged a folded bill between her thumb and forefinger. Preacher took it. They moved inside.

The third girl, a dumpy redhead said, "Got to clear our palates after a night of blow jobs."

The other girls laughed. "Imp?" Preacher said.

"Imp'll be fine," the blonde said, "but make sure it's Imp, not Old Rotgut bar whiskey. And put up three Iron's also."

Preacher poured out double shots of Imperial Whisky and three bottles of Iron City beer.

"Hey you," the little dark-haired girl said, indicating Kalinyak. "Want a party?" Kalinyak shook his head, no. "We'll give you three for two."

"What else you gonna give him," Preacher said. "If he's lucky it'll just be the clap."

"Oooh," the girl said. "Slip one, slip another, slip me, you slip your mother..."

"Oooh," the other two girls said. "Slip fight, slip fight..."

"Naw, slip fight with you girls, is be nasty to the mentally defective..."

"Do you know that German girl?" Kalinyak said to the redhead.

"Which is that?"

"You know, the German girl," Preacher said.

"Stand-offish bitch," the tall blonde said. "Yeah, I know her."

"Where I can find her?"

She looked at her girlfriends. They shrugged. "What, you in love with her?" the blonde said, laughing.

"I don't even know her," Kalinyak said.

"What about her friend?" the blonde said. "Guy's always asking for her, with the moustache?"

"Cory?"

"Yeah, what about him?"

"Yeah, I know him. What else can you tell me?"

"She's a loner, free agent," the blonde said. "Comes in every now and then. Makes her score, then we don't see her for a while. I get the feeling she lives out somewhere, maybe West Virginia, Ohio. Could be a straight housewife, you know, looking to make a little extra spending money. You a cop?"

"Not really."

"What does that mean?"

"It means not really."

"Cops been asking for her," the blonde said. "Ever since Dahlgren was killed."

"You knew Dahlgren?"

"I knew him," the blonde said.

"Good?"

"Better than good."

"What's the guy to her? Cory?" The girls didn't answer. "He her pimp?" They busied themselves with their drinks.

"What's your price?" Kalinyak said to the blonde.

She looked at Kalinyak a long time. "You have sad eyes," she said.

"Oh, please," the dark-haired girl said.

"I'm not vice. I'm not a cop. And I don't want to have sex with you..."

"We've heard that before," the blonde said.

"That's the oldest story," the redhead said. "Three things I learned never to fall for—the check's in the mail, I won't come in your mouth, and I'm not a cop ..."

The short Spanish-looking girl laughed hard. Her Iron City beer sprayed over her dress front and onto the redhead, which caused her to laugh even harder.

"Tina, come on!" the redhead said. "You're getting me soaked."

"Guys promise you the sun, moon, and the stars, and you bargain down from there," Tina said.

"I got good radar," the blonde said of Kalinyak. "I think you're all right."

"And she can't turn down a trick," the redhead said. "She's greedy."

"Older men make me want to—"

"Throw up—" the dark-haired girl said, laughing.

Preacher laughed so hard he snorted through his nose. "You cold, little bitch, you cold..."

"Who you calling little?"

"Shit, you gotta look up to a midget," Preacher said. "Take off them platform shoes, you just about disappear."

"How much?" Kalinyak said.

"Remainder of the night—two bills," the blonde said.

"Hey," Preacher said, "he don't want to buy you, he just wants to rent you for a little while."

"Watch your mouth, jigaboo," the blonde said.

"Hey, don't you go jigabooing me," Preacher said.

"Just don't be messing with my business..."

"She don't mean nothing by it," the Spanish whore said.

"I didn't know she had racist tendencies, is all."

"I call you 'jigger' all the time. That's the way we call it. What's the big deal?" the Spanish whore said.

"You a spic midget, you allowed to."

"Two hundred's fine," Kalinyak said.

"A-okay," the blonde said, putting her arm through his. "And a bottle of Imp."

The other two girls laughed. "Hey, old man, she needs to get drunk to do you..."

There was a cab parked at the curb, a gypsy job, an old Chrysler with decals that said, "Moe's Family Rides." Kalinyak and the blonde got in.

On the short ride to the hotel, the blonde opened the Imperial and drank straight from the bottle.

"I like this place," the blonde said as they walked through the empty lobby. "I've scored here from time to time." While they waited for the elevator, she gazed at herself in a mirrored pillar opposite the elevator. Moving up to his room, she said, "Let's see your money."

"I'll have to write you a check."

"Forget it."

"How about a credit card?"

"Don't be an asshole," she said. He pulled out two hundred dollar bills and handed them to her. They moved out of the elevator and down the hall to his room.

"What's your name?" Kalinyak said.

"Lara. You ever see that movie, 'Doctor Zhivago?' That's the girl's name from that movie. My mother loved that movie. My father was Russian. You ever hear of the Russian mafia? That was my father. They killed him."

"Who?"

"The communists," she said.

They entered the room. "You must have been very young," Kalinyak said.

"My mother said they shot him into little pieces."

"I'm sorry."

"I don't give a fuck. Mother said he was basically an asshole. Very big in the secret police..."

"Hm."

Neither spoke for a long moment. On the night table, Kalinyak's travel clock ticked softly. "So," Lara said

"So."

She laughed.

"That story about your father—"

"I made it up." She took another long drink from the whiskey bottle. "Look at this!" She walked to a picture of Kalinyak's daughter and held it in her hand. "She's cute. Daughter, granddaughter?"

"Daughter.

She put the picture down and began to undress. "No," Kalinyak said. "I just want to talk."

"What?"

"I want to ask you questions."

"You're weird."

"I want to talk."

"About?"

"Jack Dahlgren."

"Another weird one."

"Did you know him?"

"Knew him very well. Sick fuck. Loved money more than life. Had contempt for people. He couldn't move his mouth without lying. What else do you want to know about him?"

"Who killed him?"

"There'd be a line twice around this hotel for the people who wanted to kill him."

"This German girl, Marika?"

"It's very possible. I might have killed him, if I had the chance."

"Why?"

She didn't talk for a long moment. She was seated on the bed. She kicked off her shoes and took another swallow of whisky. "He beat me up so bad he put me in the hospital."

"Why?"

"He was going to teach me a lesson. Ah, it's a long story. He was bad. Come here." She leaned back on the bed and opened her arms. He just stood there. "You don't think I'm pretty?"

"You're very pretty. I just don't—have the heart for this kind of thing. I've seen too much. Let's put it that way."

"I've seen a lot, too."

"I'm sure you have. There was a time, but, ah...No more. What I've seen men do to women..."

"Some women deserve it."

He didn't speak. She closed her eyes. He moved to her and shook her. "What?" she said.

"I have some questions."

"Later," she said. Her breathing deepened and she was asleep. He moved to a large chair opposite the bed. He sat in it. He did not close his eyes. He stared at the pictures of his daughter.

He fell asleep in the chair. He slept badly. At some point, he felt someone tugging at his arm. He looked up. It was his daughter. She was mouthing something that he couldn't make out. "Yes, my darling," he said. "Yes. Yes."

He was awakened by the phone ringing. "Yes?"

"Kalin?"

"Who is it?"

"Gus."

"Magoczy?"

"Right."

"Father Magoczy?"

Gus Magoczy laughed at the other end of the line. "That's what they call me. I'd love to see you, Frank. I just didn't want to—"

"I wouldn't have even been here, if Bobby Mack hadn't called me," Kalinyak said. "I didn't know about Dahlgren."

"Isn't that something? We all knew, though, that— "

"Where are you?"

"Up by Altoona. I want to talk to you. I want to talk about Dahlgren. It's important. Can you drive up here? It'll take you an hour, hour and a half."

"All right."

"Lunch? How's that?"

"Okay."

"Okay. We can meet at the church— I'm at the Church of St. Ladislas—maybe better if we meet at this other place— Look, you take Route 22 out of Pittsburgh, it'll take you right here, town called Tracyville, just outside of Altoona. Eleventh Avenue and Fifth Street. Now I'll meet you at a place three blocks over. This would be on Eighth Avenue, place called Café Russniaki. Noon?"

"Sure."

"It's been a long time, Frank. Lot of stuff has gone by."

"Lot of stuff."

"I'm looking forward to this. God bless you, Frank."

"Gus, what do I say to you? God bless you, Father?"

"You could say it, but it wouldn't help."

Kalinyak hung up and tried to rouse Lara. "What?" she said, bolting upright in the bed.

"I have to go."

"Good bye."

"I can't leave you here."

"Damn. Did we screw?"

"No."

"Are you a fag?"

"No."

"Did you ask all the questions you wanted to ask?"

"What was it with the German girl and Dahlgren?"

"She was out for him, no doubt about it. She had come around specially for him."

"What do you think it was?"

"I think he probably screwed her over, as he did everyone. She was looking for revenge."

"You believe she killed him?"

"Yes, I do, but that don't mean shit. It's my opinion and opinions are like assholes, everyone has one. Could have been anyone of a thousand people. Ton of people didn't like him, including me."

"He beat you up..."

"Wanted to mess about in my life. Run things."

"Why?"

"I'll tell you some time. Maybe. Long story."

"Where can I find this Marika?"

"Told you, didn't I? Don't know where she lives. And I'm surprised she come around last night. The cops have been looking for her high and low. I'd ask that, Cory. He must know."

"He says he doesn't."

"Woman of mystery, isn't she?" She reached for the whisky bottle and took a deep drink. "She's very weird, is what I'd say."

Chapter Five

The drive to Tracyville was dreary. It had begun to rain again. The road was slick; everything was gray and soggy. From either side of the two-lane, heavy-leafed trees, dripping precipitation rose up the steep sides of the surrounding mountains, thick with tangled vines, heavy brush, and decaying logs. The thick air smelled of mold, rotting leaves, bark, trunks.

From time to time, Kalinyak would come to a bleak, soot-crusted mill town with boarded up stores and buildings, cobblestone streets, closed-down factories with rusted iron fences and gates, corrugated shutters. Everything was old and dead or dying.

He reached Tracyville at noon. He came to a narrow, murky river; a black iron bridge crossed the river and Kalinyak drove over it, his tires making a thump-thump sound as they bounced along the uneven, thick-beamed wooden road-bed. He drove past the church of St. Ladislas, a large stone building, with a rambling wooden house, the rectory, right next to it. Eleventh Avenue was lined with old dingy yellow brick buildings, a mixture of dwellings and businesses, a storefront gypsy parlor, a hair salon, a TV repair shop. Abandoned streetcar tracks criss-crossed the cobblestone main avenue.

He turned on Fifth Street and drove three more blocks to Eighth Avenue. Café Russniaki was on the corner. It, too, was built out of yellow brick, but so grime encrusted that you could barely tell its original color. A flickering neon sign in the window announced that it was open.

Kalinyak parked at the curb in front of the café. It was raining harder now, and Kalinyak had to step from the car to the sidewalk to avoid getting his shoes soaked by a narrow stream that flowed alongside the curb.

There were half a dozen people inside the bar, working folk in twill trousers and flannel shirts, overalls and denim jackets, except for a roundish, balding man at a far table. He was wearing a black suit and a priest's turned around collar. "Gus," Kalinyak called out as he approached the table.

Magoczy looked up at him with dull eyes. "Frank?" Had Kalinyak run into him unannounced on the street, he never would have recognized him. As Kalinyak remembered him, Magoczy had been thin with an angular face. His face now was pudgy and bloated, the skin blotchy and red. He had lost most of his hair. He wore thick glasses, which were fogging up in the damp tavern.

"Yes," Kalinyak said.

"Doesn't look like you."

"You've changed also. It's been, what, twenty years?"

"Maybe longer. What can I buy you?"

"I'm not hungry."

"How about a drink?"

"Do they serve food?"

"Oh, sure. Lud!" Gus Magoczy called to the bartender. A thickset man approached the table. "This is Lud Chamerek, He owns this place. Say hello to Frankie Kalinyak, old friend of mine. We call him Kalin or the Hunky Hurricane..."

"Anyone a friend of Father's here must be a good man."

"He is a good man, Lud. And you're a good man. You have to excuse me, Frank. I've imbibed."

Lud Chamerek looked at Kalinyak and nodded sympathetically. "The Father likes to indulge. Sometimes he indulges too much. We have to take him over to the rectory and put him to bed. But he has good friends here. He's a good man, he just has a problem."

"A lot of people have problems," Magoczy said. "There's a distance, you see, between, between—" He let the thought hang in the air.

"What's your pleasure? Imp 'n Iron, like the Father?" Lud said.

"Nothing to drink. How about some food?" Kalinyak said.

"I have a good *ledvinky*—"

"Fried kidneys," said Magoczy, "so good, you can barely taste the piss..."

"Best part of kidneys," Kalinyak said. "What's kidney without that piss taste?"

"You got that right," Lud said, laughing. "You a polack or what?"

"He's like me, a hunky," said Magoczy.

"Is it true what they say?" Lud said. "If you have a Hungarian, a hunky, for a friend, you never have to go looking for an enemy?"

"Trust a snake before a polack," Magoczy said. "Trust a polack before a Serb. And never trust a hunky." He laughed loud and long at that.

"My *ledvinky*, believe me, no taste like piss," said Lud. "I have my own special way to keep the taste out..."

"Piss taste or no, that's what I'll have."

"'You're out of touch, my baby...'" Magoczy said. Lud moved back to the kitchen area behind the bar.

"What?"

"Something. Don't know. It's in there," he said, jabbing one finger into his temple. "Song."

"Okay."

"A lot, Frankie, going through my mind. Can't shut it down." He had three whiskey shots lined up in front of him.

He downed the first one, neat. There were four empty shot glasses on the table.

"So," Kalinyak said. "What's up?" Magoczy nodded over his whiskey. "How's your family?"

"I'm out of touch. My brothers are all—I don't even know where they are. My mother's still alive, but she lost it. Down in Greenfield in this place, you know for old people who—" He put his hand up to his head and made a twirling motion. "Hungarian Church runs it. You know they had to get rid of the old church, St. Philomena's—"

"I heard."

Magoczy laughed harshly. "Rome decreed it was a cult, cult of St. Philomena. Did an investigation, said there were no facts known about her to justify her sainthood. Removed her from the calendar of saints."

"I heard about it."

"The old lady could never accept it. Had to go to the Hungarian church on Saline Street, St. Marek Krizin. She took a hit on that, completely unbalanced her. She still calls out to St. Philomena. She doesn't even recognize me."

"She's an old lady."

"Eighty-five something."

"That's old."

"Older than I'll ever get."

"St. Philamena's—shook me up," Kalinyak said.

"That devil Dahlgren was in on it."

"How so?"

"How so? He was the devil!" Magoczy slammed his hand down hard on the table. The silverware clattered. His eyes began to tear up. "She was a saint, Philomena! Don't let no one tell you different, Frank. They can't force me to believe lies— not the Pope even! How could they remove her from the calendar of saints?"

"It's the church. Politics."

"Politics! Naw. The Devil. How could they do this? Deveneration? Saint for hundreds of years. All the miracles in her name. There's her remains. In Rome. I seen them! They was in the catacombs, Via— Via Salaria, Saint Priscilla, they call them the Queen of the Catacombs. I been there.

You have the Hotel Romulus is over here, very nice place, and the motel Salaria, which is where I stayed."

"I remember this from school," Kalinyak said. "I remember the nuns hitting me on the hand with a ruler because I was left-handed. And I could never get all the stuff about St. Philomena straight."

"Frankie, I'm telling you, this is the fact. Young, thirteen. Virgin. They raped her, cut her with a knife. Devils! She was a *virgin*, Frankie, suffered a martyr's death. You could read the inscriptions. I been there, in Rome. 'Peace with you, Filumena.' That was in Latin, spelled her name with an 'f'. There were artifacts, all kinds in that catacomb, that tomb, engravings, a vial with her blood! The miracles begin—" Magoczy held up an arthritic hand, gnarled, distorted knuckles, and began to enumerate the miracles with his fingers: "St. John, the Cure of Ars, healer, he said *she* did the healing. Blessed Damien de Veurster, built a leprosarium after Philomena. Fray Andresito, this was in Chile, built an alter to her in the Recoleta Franciscana church. Miracle after miracle occurred in her name! Pope Gregory XVI himself declared her a saint. He instituted the feast day for her." Tears were now streaming down Father Magoczy's face. "And they claim she's not a saint! They dare to claim that? In my own life, she performed miracles."

Kalinyak didn't say anything. He felt sad and uncomfortable.

"I wanted to kill myself," Magoczy said. "Dahlgren put me in despair. And I prayed to St. Philomena, and she saved me." He wiped his tears and said very softly, almost inaudibly: "St. Philomena, pray for us. St. Philomena, filled with the most abundant graces from your very birth, pray for us. St. Philomena, faithful imitator of Mary, pray for us!"

Lud arrived at the table with the fried kidneys. Kalinyak sniffed at them. "What do you think?" Lud said.

"Nice," Kalinyak said.

"Just a little whiff," Lud said. "After all, what's *ledvinky* without a little smell, you know..." He laughed. "It's like *shmushky, pizda.* Excuse me, Father, but— you know, *shmushky* without a little tang..."

"Is not *shmushky*," Kalinyak said. Father Magoczy shook his head.

"He wouldn't know that," Lud said, laughing. "We shouldn't be talking about pussy with the good father..."

"I know about *shmushky*," Magoczy said, nodding. "I know. Jack Dahlgren taught me all about *shmushky*..."

"Well, he was good for something," Lud Chemerek said.

Kalinyak ate the fried kidneys ravenously. "Good, good," he said.

"What did I tell you," Lud said, moving off.

"How you been otherwise, Gus? Your life?"

"How could my life have been? Devoted to God? That's bullshit, you know that Frankie. I tried to make amends."

"For what? What did you want to talk about?"

"We got a lot to talk about," Magoczy said. "I got it all up here..." He tapped his forehead again, just above his eyeglasses. "Jack Dahlgren was the devil, you know."

"I think that's a little harsh. Look, I have no thing to defend Dahlgren—"

"Why you here, then?"

"Bobby Mack called me—"

"For what reason?"

"Well, Dahlgren was one of the original gang, you know that—"

"Original Huns," Magoczy said. "Remember what he used to do back in the old days?"

"He did a lot of things."

"Yes, he did. May he fry in hell." Magoczy downed the second shot glass in one gulp. "Do you think I wanted to spend my life like this?" Magoczy pushed his face very close up to Kalinyak's. He smelled strongly of beer and whiskey.

"Priest, you mean?"

"Ha, priest! Jack Dahlgren was after my soul, the son-of-a-bitch. You don't remember?"

"I remember he was always doing rotten things."

"And bringing us in on them?"

"Sometimes."

"Sometimes? What do you remember?"

"I don't know."

"You remember—"

"There were things—"

"There were things. Yeah there *were* things." Magoczy downed the last shot glass and waved Lud Chamerek over. "Give me a little more..."

"You've had enough, Father."

"Enough will be when I say enough."

"Let me take you home," Kalinyak said. 'We'll continue this tomorrow."

Magoczy threw his arms open. "It's no use." Kalinyak helped him to his feet.

"We'll talk further over breakfast," Kalinyak said. "When your mind is clearer."

"My mind. My mind!" He made the sign of the cross. Kalinyak steered him toward the door.

"You take care, Father," Lud Chamerek called after him.

Kalinyak got him outside. There was an old green Dodge parked at the curb and Gus insisted he had to drive it back to the rectory. "Naw, you're not driving. Give me the keys."

After some grumbling, Magoczy gave him the keys to the car. "Know what year this is, this car? This car's thirty-some years old. Old woman in the parish died and left it to us. It doesn't have but twenty thousand miles on it. Amazing."

Kalinyak started the car up and drove off through the rain, which was falling in thick sheets.

Magoczy fell asleep as soon as he was settled in the car. He snored softly.

Kalinyak pulled up to the curb in front of the rectory. "Gus," he said, shaking him. "Gus, c'mon, you have to get to bed."

Magoczy got out of the car and Kalinyak walked with him up the flagstone walk to the porch of the rectory. He rang the bell at the door and a dumpy, older woman opened it. "I'm an old friend of Father's," Kalinyak said. "He needs to lie down."

"He reeks," the old woman said, helping Magoczy into the rectory. "Ah, Father Magoczy, what are we to do with you?"

"God will take care of me," Magoczy mumbled.

"God will take care of all of us," the old woman said.

"I'll call him in the morning," Kalinyak said. He gave her the car keys.

"He'll be all right," the old lady said. "Whiskey priest! Something sad about that."

Kalinyak walked in the rain back to the Café Russniaki and picked up his car. He was soaked and hungry and tired. At a convenience store on the edge of town, he bought a container of coffee and a cheese danish. He checked into a motel, the Mountain Inn. The room reeked of bug spray and the wall-heating unit didn't work. He tried the television and could only bring in two local stations, and those were filled with wavy lines and snow.

He felt tired and dispirited. He had driven all this distance, and what had he learned? That his old friend Gus Magoczy was a pathetic drunk who thought Dahlgren was the Devil, and there was a certain deviousness in the sale of St. Philomena's.

He yearned to sleep, but there were too many things eating away at him. He lay fully clothed on the bed and stared up at the ceiling. Reticulations of cracked plaster formed a web and he felt somehow caught in it.

The detective in him, the pro, was trying to make some sense out of all of this. There was a dangerous, psychopathic German whore who must have had something to do with Dahlgren's death. But who was she? And what was it all about, including Dahlgren's myriad scams and questionable relationships? And what about the St. Philomena sale, which seemed to have so troubled Gus Magoczy? Did that have anything to do with Dahlgren's murder?

He called Bobby Mack on his cell phone. "I'm up here near Altoona. I was with Gus Magoczy," he said. "He called me. He's not doing good. He's just, you know, a drunk. Pathetic drunk."

"I know."

"I'm going to stay up here overnight. He wants to talk to me. I'll see how he is when he's sober."

"I had a call from that Cory character," Bobby Mack said. "Wanted to talk with you. Had something, he said. I met him at the Hot Box. Bartender told me you were there, told me what happened..."

"German hooker, Cory's friend, pulled a gun on me. She's twisted, this one is. I thought she was going to use it on me. I would bet this is our killer. Get your men out there, get her taken in. If she didn't do it herself, she damn well knows who did."

"I'm trying to put a fire under homicide. No one cares. I told you. They figure Dahlgren got what he deserved. Even the Egg doesn't seem to care. It's just you and me, Frank. We're the only ones who care. Bartender said you went back to the hotel with some chippie. You do something with her?"

"You mean sexually? I figure I've gone this long and the worst I ever had was the clap. Why tempt the gods? She knew the German girl, knew Dahlgren. Thought she might have some info, something. She only told me what we already know—Dahlgren was into beating up the pros, the working girls. She had a hey-rube with him. She thinks he beat up the German and she was getting her revenge."

"But what about that thing on the wall, you know —?"

"Your Out of Time."

"What the hell is that? Can you tell me that?" Bobby said.

"Who knows? We're not talking normality here. Who knows what they're thinking. Whoever did Dahlgren is nuts. No doubt about it. What's your read on this Cory?"

"What are you asking me for? I have no read on him. Says about the German, he barely knows her."

"I know."

"They have some kind of relationship. Maybe he pimps for her. Bartender at the club said he's interested in her, she's interested in him. They're doing some kind of business."

"Well, if he's not in with her on it, he better be very careful."

"I told him that. He says, 'Hey, I have no interest in the bitch. If I never see her again, it won't be too soon...'"

"I have some expense chits for you."

"You're coming back when?"

"Tomorrow, early afternoon."

"How about dinner?"

"Good."

"Want me to ask Theresa if she has a friend for you?"

"How about if I bring Betty Malloy? She talked about getting together."

"It'd be good."

"I'll give her a call."

"Let's meet at McGuire's, say, what? Seven?"

"Sounds good. Another thing—the blonde, the gun—she threw it into the river. Off the Ninth Street Bridge."

"I'll talk to Hanratty. They should send a diver out there, try to find it. But they don't really care."

Kalinyak hung up and called Betty Malloy. "I was just with Father Gus."

"Magpie! How is he?"

"He's a drunk; what else is there to say…"

"That's very sad. As I remember him, he was always a good guy, gallant with women, not like the usual neighborhood kid."

"I'm staying up here near Altoona overnight. I'll have breakfast with him. He didn't make much sense before. He sure has a thing about Jack—"

"Dahlgren used to always say, 'I don't know what he wants from me.' When he became a priest, I think it really spooked Jack. Jack was peculiar about the church. He was always scoffing at it and yet deep down he had the fear in him. His mother and grandmother, they really beat it into him."

"Funny how that goes. When we were kids he was always talking about the devil. We weren't all that religious, and the devil meant very little to me. I think that's why I never went all that bad. In order to sin, I think you have to have a sense of sin. I didn't have it as strong as most."

"Isn't it funny? Sarah Jo was so religious, she was going to become a nun and all of that, and she goes real bad. And Dahlgren—he told me when he was little he wanted to become a priest."

"I'm meeting Bobby Mack and his girl friend for dinner tomorrow night. How'd you like to join us?"

"I'd like that. I always liked Bobby. He's good people."

"McGuire's. Downtown. I can pick you up."

"I'll be in the downtown area. Have to be at the Hall of Records for Eggerman. I'll meet you there."

"We're going to meet at seven."

"It's nice hearing your voice, Frank. You always had this kind of nice thing in your voice. Dahlgren used to always kid about it. He was envious of you in a lot of ways."

"Envious of me?"

"You were the better athlete. You were tougher. You were smart."

"No one was smarter than Dahlgren."

"True. But he had a lot of envy in him."

"I'll see you tomorrow."

Kalinyak slept poorly. The motel was on Route 22, just outside of Tracyville, and all night eighteen-wheelers rumbled by, air brakes squealing, horns squawking. The danish and fried kidneys were sour in his stomach.

It continually snaked through his mind that coming back here was a mistake. He wasn't sure what he thought he'd find in coming home, but it didn't make him feel good.

As he tossed in the bed, feeling damp and alternately warm and cold, it occurred to him that he had no place in this world. Since his daughter had been killed, something had died in him, also—his connection to people and a life. He felt alien in Tucson and now alien in his hometown. He felt removed from everyone. His past felt as though it had happened to someone else.

Who was he? What was he doing here? His thoughts kept turning over and over in his mind, spinning, roiling. He got up to piss, feeling vaguely dizzy. He thought he would throw up.

As dawn came into the room, he rose and dressed. He brushed his teeth with his finger and soap. He stepped outside. The morning was damp. A light drizzle fell, and a bluish, smoky haze sifted through the mountains.

He checked out of the motel and drove into Tracyville. It was a bit past seven and he wondered if Magoczy would be awake. He was a priest, he reasoned, and not likely to be sleeping in.

He parked in front of the rectory and rang the bell. The dumpy woman from the day before opened the door. "Father Gus?"

"Oh, he left," the woman said.

"Left? Where'd he go?"

"Pittsburgh."

"Why?"

"I'm not sure. He received a phone call, oh, an hour or more ago."

"Who?"

"Eggerman? I think that's who called."

"Eggerman? Are you sure?"

"That's what I thought he said."

"Eggerman? Why would he be calling?"

"Maybe I have it wrong. That's what I thought he said. He had to see Eggerman."

"Where?"

"He didn't say. It worries me, this weather and all. He's not the world's best driver in good circumstances."

"Was he sober?" She made a small, embarrassed shrugging gesture, as if to say, 'how would I know?'

The drive back from the mountains was slow. The road was slick with moisture and the truck traffic was heavy. At a sharp bend, he had to brake quickly: a trailer truck had jack-knifed, hitting a van and overturning it. An ambulance, several police cars, and a tow truck protruded onto the road. Flares had been set out and a cop was directing traffic around the accident. The van had been flattened and Kalinyak wondered if anyone had lived through the crash. He looked over the crash site to make sure that Father Gus's green Dodge wasn't involved.

It was late morning when he reached Pittsburgh. As he drove along the Penn-Lincoln Parkway at the edge of the Monongahela River, his cell phone rang. It was Bobby Mack. "Jesus," he said. "Jesus, Jesus, Jesus, Frank."

"What, Bobby? You're breaking up—"

"The Egg. The Egg..."

"What?"

"Killed!"

"What?"

"Killed. Just like Jack Dahlgren."

"I didn't hear—you said killed?"

"Cut all to shit."

Kalinyak didn't speak for a long moment. He could hear Bobby Mack's heavy breathing on the other end of the phone.

"Where?"

"Out by Pine Valley. The old juke joint."

"No. No. Same, same place?"

"Two, three motels down from the last one. This is the Forester's Inn. I'm over there now. Jesus. What a mess. Jesus, Frankie. What's going on?"

Chapter Six

Kalinyak took Veteran's Bridge across the Allegheny River, then followed McKnight Road north to route 19. His mind was a blur of jumbled thoughts—Eggerman killed in the same way as Dahlgren? Did that mean that there was writing on the wall in blood!? And where was Magpie Magoczy? The housekeeper at the rectory had said he was driving to Pittsburgh to see Eggerman. And Eggerman was at a motel near Pine Valley? It was nightmarish. It made no sense. *I'm dreaming this,* he told himself.

He came to Pine Valley. The juke joint looked amazingly like it had in his youth, a white, slat board building with green doors and shutters, surrounded by tall pine trees. The sign in front was green neon in the form of a tree.

It was raining hard now. He could see down the two-lane highway, a crush of police cars. The lot in front of the Forester's Inn was jammed with them, lights flashing blue and red. There must have been twenty-five cars-- county cars, township cars, City of Pittsburgh cars.

He parked and started across the lot. A yellow wooden barrier had been set up in front of a far section of the motel. A heavy-set police photographer was lumbering around with a camera, shooting off as many pictures as he could, from as many angles as he could.

Phil Hanratty, the Deputy D.A., moved at a half-run toward a beige Ford at the corner of the lot, his hair blowing in the damp wind, his raincoat shedding pearls of water. Kalinyak, juking nimbly to avoid puddles, hurried across the motel lot to him.

They stood beneath an overhang. "This is piss poor, Kalin," Hanratty said. He took a cigarette from a crushed pack, put it in his mouth, offered the pack to Kalinyak who declined, lit up, shook his head. "Piss fucking poor. I just don't know," he said.

"Where's Bobby?"

"In there." He indicated one of the units, number 14. "I mean, okay, you cut up Jack Dahlgren, shit load of people would have liked to help you. But the Egg? All right, The Egg could be tough. He was a tough lawyer, no doubt about it. He played it hard, but he was a first-rate man. You know that. You know that better than I do. Dahlgren, as we all know, was a scum bag. Not the Egg. The Egg was the gold standard. Look, this is going to stir up people, newspapers and all that shit. You know how it goes. Let's not make a panic thing out of this. Let's play it tight to the vest. I gotta get back downtown. You talk to Bobby. He'll fill you in."

Kalinyak started into unit 14. A uniformed cop barred his way. He flashed his DA's I.D. The cop barely glanced at it. "I don't know what this is," he said.

Bobby Mack approached from inside the room. "Let him in. He's on the investigation."

The scene was almost exactly as it had been in the Dahlgren photos: Eggerman, nude, was spread-eagle on the bed; bed and floor were soaked with blood; he was bound hands and feet with black leather straps, just as Dahlgren had been. Kalinyak studied them and realized they were trouser belts. There was a gag in Eggerman's mouth, a motel hand towel. On the mirror, in large, bloody letters, was scrawled, *"Baby your out of time."* There was an hour glass on the bed stand.

Eggerman, too, had been castrated. Unlike Dahlgren, he had been awake. His eyes were round with horror.

"What is this?" Bobby Mack said. *"What the fuck is this?"*

The coroner's people were in the room. Two homicide detectives were taking measurements. A technician was dusting for prints. "Walk with me," Bobby said.

They went outside and crossed the lot to the motel office. The manager, a rail-thin, asthmatic-looking man, with a complexion the color of a week-old newspaper, sat behind the sign-in counter. He looked stricken. "He came in by himself?" Bobby said.

"Said he was looking for someone. He said Room 17, that's the room down there, where this all happened. I said, 'Who you looking for?' He said 'a man. A priest.' "

"A priest," Bobby Mack said. "Did he give you a name?"

"No, he just said he was looking for a priest. Room 17. I said I don't think there's a priest there. He just waved me off and walked down to the room."

"What time was this?" Kalinyak said.

"I don't know. Before eleven."

"Who rented the room?"

"Woman. Blonde woman."

"She have an accent?"

"Could be. She didn't talk much. She rented the room early in the morning. About nine or so she left. Then she came back."

"What time?"

"About the time the man was going to the room. I saw her hurry across the lot, and she was talking to the man outside room 17. Then they both went inside. Couple of hours later she left. I figure it was kind of, you know—we have Pine Valley over there, people meet, have drinks, come over here, spend a couple of hours. You know how that goes."

"She drive off?"

"I don't know. I saw her walk across the lot, and then I lost sight of her."

"What time does Pine Valley open?"

"They go pretty much from early morning on. It used to be strictly a night-spot and then, I don't know, four, five years ago they started to open early. They have activity pretty much all day and night."

"Let's walk over there," Kalinyak said to Bobby Mack.

Pine Valley was a couple of hundred yards back down the road. They passed the Pine Inn motel where Dahlgren's body had been found.

There were three or four cars parked at the rear of Pine Valley. One was an older green Dodge. "Jesus," Kalinyak said.

"What?"

"That's Magpie's car..."

They opened a ragged screen door and then the green entrance door. The place was dark. The ceiling was covered with myriad small lights, mimicking stars. A juke-box in the corner was an antique, from the fifties. The place smelled musty. "It hasn't changed," Kalinyak said. "From high school. Do you believe this? This is like a time capsule."

Father Magoczy was seated at the bar. They first saw his face in the smoky mirror behind the bar. The bar lighting made his face chalk white, as though he had on make-up. There were four girls seated at a side table talking in hushed tones, most likely secretaries on their lunch hour.

"What're you doing here?" Kalinyak said when they reached the bar. Magoczy barely acknowledged them. He did not speak.

"Gus" Bobby Mack said. "How you doing?"

"What?" Magoczy said dully.

"It's Bobby Mack...with Kalin..."

"Yes. Bobby. Yes. It's been a while." He was very drunk. "God bless us all," he said, crossing himself.

"What're you doing here?"

Magoczy shrugged. Reached for his drink. Raised it to Kalinyak and Bobby Mack. He drained the glass, then slipped sideways off his stool. Kalinyak caught him. He was unconscious.

"Jesus Christ," Bobby Mack said.

They carried him to a booth and laid him on the red leatherette seat. The bartender came to them, and Bobby Mack flashed his I.D. "What time did he get here?"

"A short while after we opened. Nine o'clock. What's going on? I heard there's been another, you know, another killing..."

"What did he say?"

"He was supposed to meet someone. An egg? Don't know what the hell that meant." He grinned, embarrassed. "I thought he was here to meet a woman, but I didn't want to say anything being that he's a, well you know, a priest..."

"Why did you think he was to meet a woman?" Bobby Mack said.

"Woman was here early, looked around, waiting."

"Blonde?" Kalinyak said.

"That's right."

"You remember the other guy who was killed?"

"Not really. I mean I know about it."

"He was with a blonde woman."

"I didn't know that. That took place on the night shift. I'm the day man. This was an attractive woman, blonde like you say. She came in, waited a while. Looked like she was waiting for someone. Got up and left. The priest comes in and he starts belting them back. Whew! Imp 'n Iron, he must have gone through six, seven in an hour."

They managed with great effort to get Magoczy on his feet. They walked him over to the Pine Inn and put him in a room. He kept blessing Kalinyak and Bobby Mack, weeping, and heaping accusations on himself, what a worthless human being he was.

Kalinyak and Bobby Mack managed to get Magoczy's clothes off and made him comfortable in the bed. Bobby Mack fetched a uniformed cop and sat him in front of the room. "If he wakes up make sure he stays here."

Kalinyak and Bobby Mack stood under an eave of the motel. The rain was coming down harder yet. There was an occasional flash of lightning and a loud clap of thunder. "Does Kari know about Doyle?" Kalinyak said.

"Not yet."

"I'll go to her."

"She'd be at his offices. She worked with him. Break it to her before it comes over the TV. I'll keep an eye on things here. I mentioned the gun thing to Hanratty. He was noncommittal before. Now they'll definitely have to send out divers."

"Whatever we can get."

"Definitely. What the hell could this be?" Bobby Mack said, sounding tired and helpless.

"You said Eggerman and Dahlgren had business together?"

"They did."

"Maybe they fucked the wrong guy."

"That's what you'd think. But who is this blonde woman? Why cut off, you know? What's that about?"

"We'll talk later."

"Frank, this has me spooked. I don't know what's going on here." Kalinyak was thinking the same thing. "I mean, the Egg, of all people! You couldn't find a brighter guy, a guy born to be a success. And a good guy. Despite all his brains and energy and ambition, he was a good guy."

"Yes, he was."

"With all of his pretensions and so forth— since we were little kids on Mirror Street—eight years old he was the judge! You needed to figure something out, you took it to the Egg." Bobby Mack fought tears. Kalinyak put his arm around his shoulders and held him tightly. "Look at us!" Bobby Mack said. "Grown men!!"

"He was the Egg," Kalinyak said.

"To do to him what was done! Jesus, Kalin, what's going on?"

* * *

Eggerman's law offices were downtown on Smithfield Street, overlooking Mellon Square Park. The building was a great, sleek metal-sheathed edifice, thirty stories high. Eggerman's offices occupied the top floor.

Kalinyak went through two great glass and aluminum doors to the reception area. "Mrs. Eggerman," Kalinyak said to the receptionist.

"Who should I say—?"

"Frank Kalinyak."

Betty Malloy appeared in the reception area. "Kari's back here," she said, leading Kalinyak down a long hallway. "We're having dinner later, aren't we?" she said.

"I don't think so."

"Why?"

He didn't answer her. She ushered him into a spacious wood-paneled office. Plush carpeting of deep green, thick drapes, a lighter green, conveyed a sense of quiet elegance. Even the paintings, awards, photographs of Doyle Eggerman and his family, had been hung and lit with care and a sense of design.

A large photograph of Kari and Doyle with Pittsburgh Mayor Brendan Macha occupied a section of wall behind a large desk. Kari, at the desk, remains of a Cobb Salad lunch on a tray in front of her, was on the phone. "Well, you give me the time and I'll make sure we're there..."

Betty turned to leave. "No," Kalinyak said. "This involves you."

"What?" He didn't speak. "What is it?" Betty Malloy said. Kari continued with her conversation. She smiled at Kalinyak and gestured as though to say, I'm sorry. I can't help this.

At last she hung up. "That was Budgie Moran. She was behind us a few years."

"Budgie, from Flemington Street?" Betty said. "She was a year behind me."

"Her husband's that builder, Mockton..."

"Cyril?" Betty Malloy said. "I remember him."

Well...?" Kari said, smiling at Kalinyak. He took in a breath. "What is it?" Her smile faded. "What?"

"He's dead," he said, feeling suddenly embarrassed and stupid. His voice sounded to him thin and high and silly.

"Who?" Kari said.

Betty Malloy put her hand on Kalinyak's arm. He could feel the tension in her fingers. "Doyle's been— he's been murdered..."

Neither woman spoke for a long moment. "I don't understand," Kari said very softly. She shook her head. "I just don't—what are you telling me?"

"Something's—something's—he was killed—just like Jack. Exactly like Jack."

"Oh, my God," Betty Malloy said softly.

"No. No. No," Kari said. Betty moved quickly toward her and put her arms around her. "What is he saying? What is he saying?" Kari shook her head sharply, closed her eyes. "What is he saying?"

"Someone murdered Doyle," Kalinyak said.

Kari Eggerman's eyes were wide with panic. They darted from side to side and she kept shaking her head. "What is he saying?" she suddenly screamed out. "No! Dear, God, no! No!" She grabbed onto Betty Malloy and moaned loudly. "The kids," she said, "what am I going to tell them? How am I going to tell them?"

Betty Malloy looked over at Kalinyak, her eyes filled with tears. She pulled Kari tightly into her. She shook her head with incomprehension, looking at Kalinyak, as if to ask, what is this? He shrugged and he felt immeasurably stupid and inept.

Kari's screams shredded the grace of the room.

Chapter Seven

|||

After delivering the news of Eggerman's death to his wife, Kalinyak had returned to the Pine Inn. Bobby Mack met him at the room where they had deposited Magpie. He and the green Dodge were gone.

Bobby and Kalinyak drove together up to Tracyville. As they crossed the Ninth Street Bridge they could see a team of divers working from a barge.

Father Magoszy, looking chastened and ill, sat with them in the parlor of the parish house. "I received a call from a woman early in the morning, six o'clock. She said she was calling for the Egg and he had to see me as soon as possible. She said it was very, very important. She told me to meet him at Pine Valley at nine o'clock. I didn't get there till after ten. The Egg wasn't there. I hadn't eaten. I had—a thirst..." He looked beaten, contrite.

"Did this woman say why he wanted to see you?"

"No. I had seen you, Kalin, night before. I thought it might have something do with that." He didn't speak for a long while. He was unshaven, and his face was blotched with broken veins. His hands trembled. "It pains me terribly about Eggerman, what happened to him. I feel sad and ashamed. Sad at the death of Doyle Eggerman, ashamed of—" He left what he was ashamed of hanging in the air, but Bobby Mack and Kalinyak understood what he was ashamed of.

They drove back to Pittsburgh. They had dinner with Betty Malloy at Johnny McGuire's. "A woman called for Doyle, oh, just after I got into the office," Betty said. "It must have been a little after nine. She said she had to reach him. It had something to do with Magoczy. He got on the phone, spoke with her, and then hurried out. He told me he was going to Pine Valley to see Magoczy—some emergency."

"This woman," said Kalinyak, "did she speak with an accent?"

"Yes. Yes, an accent."

Phil Hanratty entered, looking harried. He brushed rain from his hat and top-coat and hung them on a rack next to the booth. The waiter approached, and he ordered a scotch neat and a shrimp cocktail.

He opened a copy of the Post-Gazette newspaper. The headline proclaimed: PROMINENT LOCAL ATTORNEY MURDERED — RUMORS OF BIZARRE RITUAL... "Look at this, for chrissake," he said, disgusted.

"What is it?" Betty said.

"We're trying to keep certain things under our hat," Hanratty said. "It's like bailing water with a sieve."

"Was it similar to Jack's death?" she said.

"Exactly like it. That's the hell of it..." His drink and shrimp arrived. He took a quick sip of scotch, nibbled on a shrimp. "That's fresh," he said. "That's fresh shrimp. That's what I like about Johnny McGuire's. Your shrimp, your oysters, your halibut or bass, are always going to be fresh. That's good. Who wants one?"

Bobby Mack took a shrimp by its tail and dipped it in sauce. "That's good shrimp," he said, reaching for another.

"We had a report on the hour glass," Hanratty said. "Both from the same company. Manufactured in Cologne, Germany."

"Bought?" said Kalinyak.

"Bought in Ohio, St. Clairsville. At some church bazaar. Both bought the same night. Actually a whole box. A dozen."

"Does that mean we can expect a dozen murders?" Kalinyak said. "Anybody remember who bought them?"

"Lady who ran the thing said it was a woman. Young blonde. She remembered because it was such an unusual purchase—twelve hour glasses..."

"Hour glasses?" Betty Malloy said. "What is that all about?"

Hanratty shook his head. "Don't ask," he said.

"Saw the divers were out today," Bobby Mack said.

"All day," Hanratty said. "Brought up eight guns."

"Eight?"

"Handguns. One shotgun. Two rifles. Don't want to tell you how much other junk they brought up. Knives, bottles, a hand grenade."

"The gun was a 9mm," Kalinyak said.

"That's good. That narrows it down. Five of the guns were 9 mm. That seems to be the gun of choice these days. Anyhow, we'll see if we can get anything from them."

Hanratty gulped his scotch right down, ordered another. Bobby Mack decided he would have lobster. Kalinyak and Betty chose to split a chicken Caesar salad. "What was the involvement Dahlgren had with Eggerman?" Kalinyak said.

"Jack had started this throw-away paper; part of the proceeds were to go to various charities," Betty said. "When we were married, he had a variation of it. Remember Matthew Patrick?"

"Kid Dynamite," Bobby Mack said. "Middleweight. Tough guy, from Homewood. Fought for a world championship."

"Was champion of one of the alphabets for about 45 minutes," Hanratty said.

"Dirtiest fighter I ever got in the ring with."

"You fought him, Frank?"

"Sure," said Bobby Mack, "the Hunky Hurricane had his day with Kid Dynamite. South Side Market House."

"He comes out first round," Kalinyak said, "and he charges across the ring and he just lets go, full force right in the family jewels. And that was just the beginning. He was shameless!"

Bobby Mack began to laugh. He choked on a chunk of lobster. He laughed so hard tears came to his eyes. He wiped them with a napkin. "When the ref tried to separate them," Bobby Mack said, gasping for air, "he pole-axed the ref. Punched him right in the adam's apple. Disqualified him, right?"

"So Dynamite is a local celebrity," Betty said. "Big with the blacks out in Homewood, Brushton. Dahlgren starts the Matthew Patrick Foundation. Going to do good works in the ghetto. Only good works, as far as I could tell, were the funds that Kid Dynamite and Jack divided up. And I'm sure he even cheated Patrick. He had discussed a similar situation with Doyle—didn't tell him it would be a scam. I said to Doyle, 'look this is my ex-husband. I'm on to this one. You be careful. Doyle.' Of course, you couldn't tell him that sort of thing—"

"Smartest man in any room," said Hanratty. "Didn't make 'em any smarter than the Egg."

"Doyle agrees to be on the board. It's the Doyle Eggerman Educational Foundation. Well, turned out, as I knew it would, that it was pure Jack Dahlgren scam-o-la. No proceeds except what went into Jack's wallet. When the Egg found out, he was livid. They had a knock-down, drag out argument, oh, this was four weeks ago, just before Dahlgren.... Dahlgren was screaming about how he had finally turned his life around, Doyle's screaming back that he hadn't turned anything around, unless it was the bank accounts and wallets of some gullible people."

"What were the charities that Dahlgren was supposed to be assisting?

Betty took a sip of white wine. "One was a home for homosexual teen-agers. Another, for runaway girls. They received nothing. Another was supposed to assist former prostitutes. And I think Magpie's church, St. Ladislas, up near Altoona"

"And none of them got anything?"

"Not a red cent. All went into Dahlgren's pocket. Can I try a bite of that?" Betty asked, indicating Bobby Mack's lobster. She laughed demurely. "I suppose that's not classy." He passed her a chunk on a fork. "Hm, that is good."

"The best seafood in the city," Hanratty said.

Betty smiled at Kalinyak and he thought, God, she's lovely. She hasn't changed a bit since high school! He knew why he had been so taken with her in those days. If it hadn't been for Dahlgren and other things, well, maybe...

"What are you thinking?" Betty said. He shook his head and smiled back. She took his hand and gave it a squeeze. "You look sad, Frank. Don't be sad..."

* * *

They had to delay Doyle Eggerman's funeral while the coroner examined the body. Because of the prominence of the deceased, exceptional care was taken. It was Saturday morning when the Egg's earthly remains were released.

Most of the important business and political figures of the city were at the funeral home, Bruno Pisek's on Saline Street, including the Alderman in the area, Milan Wychek, who had a nice piece of the business. He had a piece of a number of Greenfield businesses—an insurance agency, a construction company, a beauty parlor. Any business that had business with the city—and which business didn't?—had at some time to come to Wychek, and when they did come to him they very often left a chunk of their operation with him. "What a mind the Egg had!" Wychek proclaimed to Kari. "Man was a genius, pure and simple. He's going to be sorely missed."

Doyle Eggerman's kids were there, two tall, strapping boys and his daughter, a serious, handsome young lady. They had come in from college, the boys from Florida, the girl from Boston. Betty Malloy's sons could not make the funeral; they both played football for Penn State, and they had a major game against Notre Dame that weekend.

Father Augustus Magoczy, Magpie, had not shown up for the funeral.

There was a steady stream of old-timers who paused to pay respects not only to the widow and her children, but also to Greenfield Bobby Mack. They talked about his father, Big Greenfield Bobby and how proud they were of the Egg and Little Greenfield Bobby. Wychek, the Alderman—he had been Alderman in ward 15, Greenfield and Hazelwood, going back to the days when Kalinyak was still in Pittsburgh—raved about Big Greenfield Bob. "There was a man could play politics like a fiddle! He made music come out of wards and elections and so forth. He never held office, but, oh, the chits that had to be paid to Big Greenfield Bob! And you're a chip off the old, whatever—" Wychek must have been eighty, but his posture was ramrod straight and his step was jaunty and his eyes clear. There was a strong odor of Aqua Velva and bourbon about him.

Later they all drove out to Calvary Cemetery where the burial took place, not far from the neighborhood in which Eggerman had been born and raised. At the graveside, Father Gilchristie, formerly of St. Philomena's, spoke, and remarked how far the Egg had traveled in accomplishment and yet how short the distance was from his birth to his death. He talked of the early days at St. Philomena's, playing baseball on the rocky field above the coal shaft. He elaborated on the coal shaft in his talk—a symbol of faith, hard work, cooperation, the closeness of the community, digging. He mentioned, as an afterthought, that it made a buck for the church.

He talked also of the demise of St. Philomena's—how its namesake had been banished from the liturgical calendar in 1961 and the effect that it had had on everyone.

A number of people rose to speak. Kalinyak was impressed at how important the Egg had become. Even the Mayor was there, Brendan Macha, from Hazelwood. He had gone to Allderdice with the Huns, and St. Philomena's before that. He was three years younger than Kalinyak.

The Mayor got up and said he would say a few words and went on for nearly a half hour, on and on about Doyle, how important he had been to the city, how the Democratic Party would miss him, the good works he performed not only in the city, but the county as well. Kari wept softly while her kids comforted her.

The Chief of Police, Stupka, a tall, solidly-built man, spoke of the horrific crime that had visited their community. "A madman is among us," he said, "and he must be found and stopped. This abomination—and I can't give details for obvious reasons—must be rectified." He made no mention of Jack Dahlgren and the abomination visited on him.

After the funeral, Kalinyak, Bobby Mack, the Pittsburgh politicos, a number of the Mirror Street Aces, and Betty Malloy accompanied Kari and her kids to the great house on Woodbine Road, North of Forbes. The Mayor, flanked by Alderman Wychek and the Chief of Police, spoke softly to Kari while the kids looked on. Kalinyak strained to hear what he was saying. He could make out that the Egg's death was a great loss.

The Mayor turned to leave, spotted Bobby Mack and Kalinyak, and walked to them. "This is a great loss," he said to Bobby Mack. "A great loss. Doyle was a treasure for the city."

"Yes," said Wychek behind him.

"We'll take care of this, won't we?" Mayor Macha said, glancing over at Police Chief Stupka.

"We'll leave no stone unturned."

"Bobby Mack," he said, "You were very close to Doyle—"

"Very close, Mr. Mayor."

Macha smiled. "Bren, okay? We've known each other long enough."

"Okay, Bren," Bobby Mack said.

"Kalin?" the Mayor said. "I heard you were in town. Doing some work for us?"

"He's helping with the investigation, "Stupka said.

"He's a good man," the Mayor said. "I still remember him from football—"

"Is that right?" Stupka said.

"Oh, yes," said Wychek. "These boys were all part of the Greenfield crowd. Bobby Mack's father organized them. They were putting up political posters before they could barely walk."

"Tearing them down, too," Bobby Mack said with a dry laugh.

"Oh, sure. That's part of the game. What was it your father always said?"

"'Let your conscience be your guide'," Bobby Mack replied.

"And truer words were never uttered!" They all laughed at that. "We were all neighbors and classmates," Mayor Macha said. "I was from Hazelwood Avenue, they were from around Mirror Street. We all went to St. Philomena's and then to Allderdice. They were a few years older." Macha turned to Kalinyak. "You've been in Arizona, haven't you?"

"That's right."

"Police work?"

"I'm retired now."

"Moving back here?"

"I don't know."

"You and Doyle were very close, as I recall."

"We were good friends."

"Tragic, tragic. Anyone have any theories?"

"Something to do with Jack Dahlgren," Stupka said.

"Is that a fact? Dahlgren? There was a rotten egg for you..."

"This is his ex-wife," Bobby Mack said, putting his arm around Betty Malloy's shoulder.

"Well," said the Mayor. "Betty, right? Malloy?"

"Yes."

"I knew your father and your brothers. I knew Jimmy Flynn, cousin wasn't he?"

"Yes, he was."

"You were not far behind our class—"

"That's right."

"Shame we're all getting together like this on such an occasion. I didn't mean Dahlgren was a bad guy. He was very likeable—"

"You don't have to apologize," Betty said. "He was just as you said, a rotten egg..."

"You're amazing, Bren," Bobby Mack said.

"How's that?"

"Names. You remember every one's name. Even in grade school."

"He's a born politician," Wychek said.

"I was always good with names," the Mayor said.

"Did you train yourself for that?" Betty said.

"God given talent. That's about it. Well, I've always been interested in people. If you're interested in something, you'll remember it. Well, I have to be off. Busy day tomorrow. We're opening a new supermarket out in West Mifflin. Early in the morning, to catch the people before they go to work..."

"When's the election?" Kalinyak said. Everyone, including Betty, looked uncomfortable.

"Not till next year. But you can't let yourself think that way. It's ABC, Always Be Campaigning..."

"At funerals?" Betty said.

"Funerals, weddings, Sheeny bar mitzvahs. ABC..."

"What's your plans after the Mayor's office?" Bobby Mack said.

Macha glanced at Wychek. "How does Governor sound?" Wychek said. "Or Senator. Sky's the limit here. He's young, relatively speaking, 45—that's young. Personable. Popular in the community. Ton of friends."

"Doyle and I talked about it often. Where we would go from here— I say 'we'—we were a team."

"We're going to miss Doyle," Wychek said. "After they made him, they broke the mold."

"What dealings did he have with Dahlgren?" Kalinyak said.

"That's for another time, another place," Wychek said. "They had their dealings. Everyone knew it. Some resented it. We'll talk about all that. Some other time."

The Mayor, Wychek, and Chief Stupka started off. The Police Chief returned to Doyle. "I'm putting a whole shitload of men on this thing. Dahlgren was one thing, good riddance a lot were saying. But not the Egg. We gotta wrap this up. I'll talk to Hanratty in the morning. Whatever you guys feel you need. The Mayor's in with me on this. Well, you heard. He and Doyle went way back."

"Doyle was a major contributor."

"That, too." Stupka winked and moved off, hurrying to catch up with the Mayor and the Alderman.

"Bendan Macha," Kalinyak said. "Who would have thought it?"

"One of the world's great jagoff's," Bobby Mack said. He looked over at Betty. "Excuse my French."

"Oh, no. I remember him from Allderdice. Jagoff big time."

"Wychek helped make him. I didn't want to have anything to do with it," Bobby Mack said. "My father despised him. If he would have been alive, Macha couldn't have made dog catcher. But, you know, I don't have the patience for this petty shit. What? Am I going to fight Alderman Wychek who's been around since the great flood? And I don't mean the '36 flood, I mean Noah's flood..."

People drifted off. Kalinyak and Betty Malloy and Bobby Mack sat with Kari and the kids for a long while. A few of the Mirror Street Aces hung on, "Buddha", Tino Bronk. Then they departed and it was Bobby Mack, Kalinyak, and Betty Malloy with Eggerman's widow and his kids. "This is a nightmare," Kari said. She began to weep softly. "It has something to do with Jack Dahlgren," she said finally. "I'm certain of it. I would always tell him, get Dahlgren out of our lives. Where was Magpie? I didn't see him there."

"He was in no shape," Bobby Mack said.

"That bad?" said Kari.

"Very bad."

"What's that?" one of Eggerman's son's said.

"Oh, Gus Magoczy. Old friend."

"Became a priest," the other son said. "I remember him. He always smelled of Iron City."

"Well, he still does," Bobby Mack said. "Hey, we all take a drop every now and then. With him, it's become a flood."

"Whiskey priest," Kari said.

"Even his housekeeper says it," Kalinyak said. "I was up there near Altoona. They all know him up there. It's pathetic."

"How do you figure—?" Betty Malloy said.

"Genetic, more'n likely," Bobby Mack said. "His father died a drunk. Oh, Gus wasn't even in grade school. And the old lady, she liked her booze. Drank it straight, too."

"Funny thing, they were always very religious." Kalinyak said.

"It is funny. It goes that way," Bobby Mack said.

Kari stood. "I'm going to try to get some sleep," she said.

"We'll talk to you tomorrow," Bobby Mack said. Each in turn hugged Kari and embraced the kids.

"We'll have breakfast," Bobby said to Kalinyak after they left the house and were standing in the red brick parking area. "I'll call you." He kissed Betty Malloy on the check, shook Kalinyak's hand, got into his Town Car and drove off.

Kalinyak and Betty Malloy stood in the driveway. A thick fog had moved in on Woodbine and the surrounding mansions. It was cold and damp and a chill went through Betty. She shivered. "Want to get something, coffee or something?" Kalinyak said to her.

"Only thing open this hour would be Politos on Forbes Street," she said. "Forbes and Shady."

"I know where it is." He put his arms around her. He could feel her shivering beneath his hands.

"I have a chill," she said. "What is it, Kalin? What's happening? First Jack, now Doyle."

"Something," he said.

"What? What is it?"

"Strange," he said. He felt stupid that he didn't have a better answer.

"It sure is," she said. "It's very weird. Scary. Two men murdered like that? At Pine Valley! We were going to drive up there before—"

"Well. Don't let it get to you."

"How do you not let it get to you? It's so awful..."

"That it is. It's very scary. We'll get whoever's done this."

"You're working with them on it?"

"Yes."

"Good. I feel good about that. I always felt when we were kids that you could take care of things." He laughed and shook his head. "You were older. We looked up to you. You were very strong."

Kalinyak felt stupid and embarrassed and didn't quite know what to say. The fact that anybody looked up to him seemed absurd. If they had only known what he had gone through the last twenty years, the stupid ways he had behaved. "I'm basically a screw-up now," he said.

"No."

"Okay. No. I'm very accomplished. I'll see you at Politos."

Though it was not yet ten, Forbes Street was deserted. It had begun to drizzle, a fine mist. Kalinyak parked at the curb in front of the restaurant. It had not changed since high school, he was thinking. Black marble façade. Stark neon: "Politos Mediterranean Cuisine." He couldn't tell if it was still open.

Betty pulled up behind him and he got out and leaned in at her car window. "I don't think it's open," he said.

"Oh, they're open," she said, getting out of her car. "Don't you remember? It always looked like it was closed. It's that black front."

Kalinyak followed her in through the front door. The dining room was off to the right, a dark bar and lounge occupied the center of the place. An elderly woman met them with menus and led them into the dining area.

"Lucy, do you remember this guy?" Betty said.

"Oh, sure. It's Frankie Kalin."

"You remember me?"

"The Hunky Hurricane? How could I forget? And you played football with my Ronnie."

"That's right. Ronnie Polito. How is he?"

"Dead, oh, five years ago. Car crash... Boulevard of the Allies. You know, he—" She mimed taking a drink. "He'd close up here and he'd, you know, he had a whole bar here, him and his friends. You all used to, even when you were kids. I remember alla yuns, way back even, playing ball at St. Philomena's..."

"Above the coal mine," Kalinyak said.

"Oh, yeah. Some ball field."

"Football, you'd get chunks of coal in your arms and legs. Ronnie was a good ball player."

"Oh, sure. Had a football scholarship to West Virginia. After Clarion."

"Didn't know that," Kalinyak said.

"Didn't take it. Loved the restaurant."

"Amazing," Kalinyak said to Betty after they were seated. "Place hasn't changed one little bit. Lucy I wouldn't have recognized."

"Ronnie's death aged her."

Betty ordered a glass of white wine, Kalinyak an O'Douls. "You're a serious non-drinker," Betty said.

"I got into trouble," Kalinyak said.

"Good that you recognized you had a problem."

"My daughter never approved of my drinking."

"You've gone through some very tough times," she said.

He didn't speak for a long while. Their drinks arrived. He stared at the O'Doul's label. "Yeah," he said at last. "You lose the kid, but you also lose yourself."

"What do you mean?"

"I'm not really here."

"That's silly."

"No. It's true. I'm like—it's like—I'm dreaming my life...That's the best I can put it."

He continuing staring at the O'Doul's label, as though it contained some arcane secret, as though the secret of life and death were there. If he could just penetrate to the heart of the label...

"What are your plans?"

He shook his head. "You mean besides finding out who killed Jack and Doyle? That's all I have now. That's my life. That's as far as my plans go. Find out who killed Jack and Doyle."

They didn't speak for a while. They sat lost in thought. "St. Philomena's," Kalinyak said at last. "A lot of memories there. Must have been the only church with its own coal mine. What became of the mine?"

"Closed years ago."

"Kids, we used to sneak in there."

"Jack told me."

"Some times we had there, St. Philomena's— sisters used to whack the hell out of me—"

"You and Jack."

"Jack? First the sisters, then Father Stan, then back to the sisters. Didn't do any good."

"I'll bet he went to confession regularly."

"He couldn't go enough..."

They both laughed at this.

"Taking her off the calendar of saints, whatever, desanctification, affected so many people," Betty said.

"The sale—"

"You know, Jack was involved in that," she said very quietly.

"How?"

"I don't know. But he was involved." She had a second glass of wine, drank it down quickly. "I better get home," she said, rising.

"I wish—" he said.

"What?" He couldn't find the words. "That you felt something?" she said.

He looked at her, startled and embarrassed. "Yes," he said.

"Don't force it, Frank. It'll come back."

"I like you a lot," he said. "I always did."

"I know. And I always liked you. If you had stayed in Pittsburgh—who knows?"

He paid the check and walked her to her car. They kissed. It was soft, quiet. It meant almost nothing to either of them. "Some day, maybe," she said.

"I hope so."

She drove off. Kalinyak stood in the soft rain, feeling infinitely lost.

Chapter Eight

He was exhausted, but knew he could not sleep. Where should he go next? He had to remain in motion. The rain had increased. He drove aimlessly for a while, then steered the car toward downtown and the Hot Box. You could barely see the neon sign through the downpour. He had to run from the car to the entrance to keep from getting soaked.

The place was filled with men, many of them middle-aged in wash-and-wear suits, guts overhanging belts, shirts and jackets stained with sweat. "Fucking coppers. All day," Preacher said, disgusted. "Killed the business. Who wants to hang out with this type people. No one gives a shit about a cop, not even their wives."

Kalinyak recognized a detective who had been on duty when he visited Bobby Mack's office. "Hey," the detective said, waving a bottle of Iron City at Kalinyak.

"Hey," Kalinyak said.

"Going from bad to worse, want my opinion. Murder's never fun," the detective said. "I've heard of some crazy stuff. This is the craziest. I'm a year from retirement. This one might have put me over the edge."

"Bad business."

"Terrible, terrible. I knew the Egg. Good man." The detective took a long swallow of beer. He grinned at Kalinyak. "Enough to turn a man to drink."

Kalinyak turned his attention to Preacher. "I take it the blonde hasn't been around."

"I'd say you're a perceptive motherfucker. She may be nuts, but she's not that nuts. You ain't never gonna see her no more. Unless that asshole can lure her out, the fag banger."

"Fag banger?"

"You knew the dude. He brought you in here. Her boyfriend. What's his motherfucking name?"

"Cory?"

"Cory."

"Fag banger?" Kalinyak said.

"Big time. Hustles the boys. They don't come across, threatens them or kicks the shit out of them. Psycho bad-ass, is what he is. Running the okay-doke with the German broad. Shit, whatever she's into, he's neck deep in it."

Kalinyak leaned close to Preacher and slipped him another twenty. "She comes around, you'll call me. You still have the number?"

"I got the number."

Kalinyak walked the few blocks over to Smithfield and the Aida Club. He peered through the window. There was no one at the bar. He entered, squinting his eyes until they adjusted to the dark. Seated at a rear table, he spotted Cory by himself, nursing a beer. He looked glum. "This is a disaster, this killing," Cory said as Kalinyak reached the table. "Going to put everybody out of business. Fucking everybody upset. Coming down on everybody. Came in here earlier, tossed the whole damn joint. Scared the boys off. Even the chippies over at the Hot Box. No one's coming out."

"Where's Marika?"

"What are you asking me that for? I barely know the bitch! Everyone thinks we're tight. I dipped her a couple a times, while back, just a little rush thing. She gave it up, no charge. Okay. I knew she wanted to work me on some scams. Okay, but she was too mysterious for me, too weird. Here today, gone tomorrow. Who needs that shit? Now they're trying to say she offed two old guys. Hey, maybe she did, maybe she didn't. I don't know anything about it. Can you buy me a beer?"

Kalinyak signaled to the bartender. "I'm broke," Cory said. "I admit it. This murder thing has just shut down everything."

"You know where she lives, don't you?"

"No, I don't."

"I think you're shitting me."

"Hey, that's your prerogative." The bartender arrived with an Iron City beer and a shot of Imperial Whiskey. Cory threw back the whiskey, nursed the beer. "The bitch is something else. I don't know why I even got involved with her," he said. "In her own world. Just doing her own thing. I don't know a damn thing about her. I thought she was from West Virginia. Then someone said she was from up around Zelienople. Someone else told me she was from Altoona."

"Altoona?"

"Said she was a religious whacko."

"Who told you that."

"One of the ladies of the Hot Box who knew her."

"Lara?"

"Lara? Tall blonde? Yeah, she told me that. She said she lived up in Altoona and was a religious freak."

"She said that?"

"That's right."

"Where can I find Lara?"

"You ain't gonna find her at the Hot Box these days. You might try the hotel bars. Sometimes she works out of there. Or the Strip area. You know, she comes from a prominent family."

"Really?"

"Father works in the D.A.'s office. Big politico mucky-muck. You ever hear of Greenfield Bobby Mack?"

"Yeah."

"That's her father..."

"Jesus," Kalinyak said. "Holy Christ."

"What?"

"I've heard of her father."

"Freak, big time, you know?"

Kalinyak felt queasy inside. He ached for his old friend. Bobby Mack had said his daughter was a junkie-hooker. But to have met her face to face. To have slept in the same bed with her. What if they had done the deed, made the beast with two backs—his good friend's daughter? "Damn," he said out loud.

"She's a sneaky one, junkie twister. Knows more than she lets on. She pretends that this Marika is nothing to her. I don't believe that. I always thought they had something going."

"Like what?"

"Damned if I know. Maybe they're both lezzies. I just don't know. But they got something between them. Come on, walk me over to the Hot Box. Maybe she's there..."

"I was just there. Wall to wall cops."

"This is a tragedy," Cory said. "What am I going to do with my life? Hey, can you put me up at your place."

"No."

"Don't take offense. It's not like I'm some fairy gonna rape you."

"No offense taken. I just don't want to know you that well."

"I thought we were friends."

"We're not," Kalinyak said. "We're nothing to each other."

"That's cold, man."

"That's the way it is."

"Well, I gotta run," Cory said. He looked nervously up and down the bar. "Gotta *move*. I'll find a place. Maybe come across Marika."

"You think so?"

"Naw, not with every cop in the Burg looking for her. I'll find someone."

"If you see her, call me. And, hey…I wouldn't spend time alone with her…"

"Why not?"

"I think she has some issues with men."

"She hates men."

"I'd say so."

"Dahlgren had it coming. Kicked the living shit out of her."

"But not this latest one."

"How do they know it's the same killer?"

"Oh, they know."

"Well, you know some shit I don't know."

"I guess I do."

Cory stood. He swayed in front of Kalinyak. "Thanks for the Imp n' Iron."

"You watch yourself…"

"Watch myself? What kind of freak do you think I am?" He laughed and moved unsteadily out of the place.

Kalinyak went to the bar. "Where will he be going?" he said to bartender.

"He usually picks up a trick. With this latest killing, though, things have been slow."

"He must stay someplace…"

"He has this girlfriend…"

"German girl?"

"You know her?"

"I met her once."

"She come in here looking for him one day. When I told him, I got the feeling he knew exactly where to find her."

"Do you know where?"

"I had the feeling it was up north some place. Oil City maybe."

"Oil City. Why do you say that?"

"She called for him once. Left a number. Area code was up around Oil City."

"Not Altoona or Zelienople?"

"No, this was Oil City."

"So if he's looking for a trick…"

"Probably in his car, cruising around the Strip. Cops have laid off over there. Political thing. Mayor's family owns a lot of shit over there. They got some places over in that area."

"Like what?"

"A fag & faghag joint, Hard Luck Club right on Penn Avenue. He sometimes hustles there. He has friends over there. I think he met the German girl there."

"What kind of car does he have?"

"Has this old, beat-up junker. Old Chevy. Blue. Peeling paint. He'll pick up some guy and they'll go at it right in the car. You know, there's the bluff there round Vickeroy Street. He'll do business there in that lot just above the boulevard."

"How do you know all this?"

The bartender lit a cigarette. Thought for a moment. "Sometimes I'll fix it up with him. He'll throw me a few bucks. Why? You interested?"

"I'm interested in him."

"This guy's trouble. Someone's going to do him good some day. He's what you might call a predator. You be careful with him."

"I will. I thank you."

"I mean, you want a nice, clean guy, I can fix you up…"

"No. No thank you. I appreciate your thoughtfulness, though…"

Kalinyak left the club and drove along Liberty Avenue to the Strip area. The Strip, northeast of Downtown, had at one time been a factory and warehouse district. There was a large produce market. Kalinyak remembered as a kid the shanty towns that occupied the area between the river and Polish Hill.

The market was still there, but the factories had long since been converted to stores, restaurants, and bars, with some loft apartments scattered throughout. He drove up Liberty Avenue, then turned off at 22nd Street, past the not-yet-open produce market, heading toward the Allegheny River. He turned again on Penn Avenue. He could see above him on the right the domes of the Immaculate Heart of Mary

Church on Polish Hill. To his left was St. Stanislaus Kostka Church, set right in the middle of the produce market.

He drove past a number of bars--Bert's Tavern, The Silver Knife, Bar Sinister, End of the Line. At the corner of Penn and 29th Street, he saw Hard Luck Café, an old-style Pittsburgh tavern in a three-story brick row house. He turned down 29th Street, which was deserted. A car was parked midway down the block, an old blue Chevy with peeling paint.

He pulled to the end of the block and parked on the same side of the street as the Chevy. He could observe it in his rear view mirror.

It was nearly midnight. Occasionally several young, flighty men would come traipsing out of the bar. Sometimes there were women with them. He couldn't believe that the police weren't watching the place. Must be crawling with undercover cops, he thought.

He was tired. He had the radio on, tuned to a national talk show that specialized in information for over-the-road truck drivers. He fought not to fall asleep. He thought of Bobby Mack's daughter and his own dead daughter, and he was filled with despair. Where was his life going?

Now he saw a couple walking down the street. He recognized Cory by the swagger of his walk. A blonde woman was with him. The street was dark. He couldn't make out her features. They both got into the beat-up Chevy. It drove off, past Kalinyak.

Was the girl Marika? If so, how had the cops missed her?

He waited a long moment and then started up his car and followed after the Chevy, staying at a distance. The Chevy turned onto Smallman Street, heading back toward Downtown. It cut cross-town toward Fifth Avenue. There was a steep hill heading up to the bluff. He saw the red of the car's taillights bumping up the cobblestone street.

He drove slowly up the street. To his left was a row of brick tenement buildings, to his right, a large empty lot. The Chevy had pulled into the far end of the lot. Scattered over the lot were discarded remnants of furniture, appliances, chunks of junked vehicles, tire rims, shredded seats, a rusted undercarriage.

He parked his car and made his way across the lot. Ahead of him, he could see the lights of houses across the Monongahela River on Mt. Washington. To his right was a steep drop down the side of the Bluff. A switchback of rickety wooden stairs criss-crossed down the side of the cliff to the boulevard below.

He came to the rear of the car. Cory and the blonde were in the backseat, having sex. She had not undressed, just pulled her panties to one side. He could not see her face.

He moved to a spot behind a burnt-out truck bed. He waited a long while. He watched the lights across the river. Occasionally a barge would make its way up the river. Cars moved across the Liberty and 10th Street Bridges. The night was cool and damp.

He was seized by an enormous sense of loss and isolation. What was he doing here? What horrific world had he descended into? How had his old friends, Dahlgren and Doyle Eggerman, come to such nightmarish ends? Where was it all leading?

An overwhelming sense of dread came over him. Ever since the death of his daughter, nothing had been right for him. He was lost, lost. He wished now he had somehow been able to carry his gun with him. He would have to talk about it with Bobby Mack. He would need a gun.

And there were others things they would have to discuss.

He heard a noise coming from Cory's car, a woman yelling. The door on the opposite side swung open and he saw the woman stagger from the car. Cory was right behind her, punching at her. Crying hysterically, she yanked away from him and started running across the lot. Cory started up the car to go after her.

She disappeared over the edge of the Bluff, running down the stairs. The car changed direction abruptly and sped off down the cobblestone street at the head of the lot.

Kalinyak bolted for the steps, ran down them. A hundred feet below, he could see the blonde leaping, falling, sliding down the steps. He charged after her, took the railing at a switchback and jumped to the landing below. She was now twenty feet ahead of him.

He continued on, stumbling after, caught her just on the edge of the boulevard, turned her to him.

Her face was streaked with tears. There was a bruise forming just below her left eye. There was a smear of blood coming from the corner of her mouth.

It was Bobby Mack's daughter, Lara.

Chapter Nine

|||

She sat in the chair opposite his bed. He had ordered up a bottle of J&B scotch. She couldn't stop crying. She was trembling. He had washed the blood off her face and used the scotch as disinfectant. "That motherfucker, that motherfucker," she kept saying over and over. "Look, I know what you think—"

"Okay."

"You think I'm a strung-out junkie..." She fished in her coat pocket for something. She found a half-smoked cigarette. She lit up. "Motherfucker took my purse...In this world, you know, can't trust anyone. I thought he was my friend..."

"What happened?"

"He found me in the Hard Luck. Asked me if I wanted to work. Took me in his car, you know? Fucked me. Wouldn't pay. Grabbed my purse. Began to beat me. Motherfucker. How'd you get there?"

"I was looking for the German girl."

"Ah. Everyone's looking for her. Killed this other guy, huh? I knew this guy."

"I know you did."

"How'd you know that?"

"He was a friend of mine. Your father is a good friend of mine."

She looked long at him. He saw a flash of anxiety in her eyes. "Who are you?"

"Ever hear him talk about Kalinyak?"

"Frankie Kalin? That's you? But you're a cop out west somewhere..."

"When Jack Dahlgren was killed, your dad called me to come back."

"Don't tell him about this. I mean, he knows all about me. He knows. But still..."

"What's happened to you is tearing him apart."

"I doubt it."

"I'm sure it is."

"I'm sorry. He wasn't the best father in the world..."

"He loves you."

She didn't speak for a long moment. "I know," she said. "When I was sixteen and hated everything about my life, and was going in wrong ways, everyone told me, don't play with fire. But I was born to play with fire. It was part of me. I wanted to set the whole world on fire."

"Where can I find Marika?"

"I don't know."

"Cory said the two of you were friends."

"Not really. She's not the kind that can have friends."

"Why not?"

"She's cold as a snake. She's scary."

"Cory said that you said she lived up in Altoona. Was a religious freak."

"She talked to me once about this priest up there. I knew him. I asked her why she was interested in him. She said she wanted to see him. It was a question of absolution."

"Absolution?"

"That's what she said."

"This priest—"

"—was my father's friend. Magoczy?"

"Yes."

"You know him?"

"Yes."

"You were all Mirror Street Aces. And Huns."

"You know about that?"

"When I was little , my father told me stories."

"I had a daughter. I told her stories, also."

"What happened to your daughter?"

"She's dead. Murdered."

"I'm sorry."

"How did you come to Magoczy?"

"A few years back, he tried to help me. But he was a lush himself. What could he do for me?"

"Did Marika hook up with him?"

"I don't know. I thought maybe she did. I'm not sure. I couldn't understand how she knew him. I figured she lived up there around Altoona. I knew she didn't live in the Burg." She began to weep again. "What am I going to do now? I'm strung out...He took all my money..."

"How much do you need?"

"A hundred. That'll get me straight so I can go out and work for my next score."

Kalinyak took some bills from his pocket and passed them to her. "Thank you." She put the bills in her bra. She stared at the red ash end of her cigarette. "I hate myself," she said so softly Kalinyak barely heard her.

"How long have you known Cory?"

"He came on the scene, I don't know, a few months ago. He's from upstate somewhere. I never had a problem with him. These two killings have just turned everything upside down. It's tough hustling out there. The hustlers are beginning to eat each other up."

"He brought Marika to you?"

"No. No, I knew her a while before I met him. She's been on the scene a while. I might have introduced them. I guess he had heard about her. He asked me about her."

"Were they close?"

"Not really. I had the feeling that maybe they were using each other. He had his scams, she seemed to have hers. No, they operated separately. I mean, I don't know when they were together what went on, but—they weren't close."

"Do you think he's involved in these killings?"

"Honestly, no. I wouldn't have thought he had that kind of violence in him."

"Until tonight?"

"Yes. He always seemed sweet, passive, lost."

"The bartender at the Hot Box said he was a fag banger..."

"Preacher said that?"

"Yes."

"I never saw that side of him."

"And Marika?"

"I could believe most anything about her. Crazy woman. Crazed."

"Why don't you sleep?"

She stood. "I have to take care of business," she said. She walked to the door. "Don't tell my father."

After she had left, he stared for a long time at the picture of his own daughter. Inside, he felt a desolation so immense that he wondered if he could go on.

The phone was ringing. Gray light spilled into the room. He had fallen asleep fully dressed. It was Bobby Mack. "I think we should talk to Magoczy again," Kalinyak said. "The German girl was trying to reach him."

"How do you know that?"

"It's a long story. Look, I'm going to need some money. I've been passing the bucks around."

"We'll cut you a check for expenses. Go full court press. The Mayor, D.A., Hanratty—they all want this thing broken."

"I take it they've had no luck finding the German..."

"They've had luck. Not the right luck. Every blonde woman with an accent who's come anywhere near the downtown clubs has been hauled in. I think they've had four Polacks, a Hunky, a Swede, and two Russians. No German."

"This Marika could be anything. They say she's German."

"The women hauled in weren't her, believe me. These could have played linebacker for the Steelers."

"What about the places on the Strip?"

"This gets a little dicey here. Mayor's family owns a lot of those joints. They're moving much more cautiously there. Don't want to ruin business." Bobby Mack exhaled. "Way of the world, we know this." His voice was barely audible.

Bobby Mack picked up Kalinyak at the hotel, and they re-visited the downtown clubs, the Aida and the Hot Box. Then they drove over to the Strip places. Downtown, up to Polish Hill, beyond the black Hill District, was carpeted with detectives canvassing in twos and threes, trying to work up any leads they could. The Post-Gazette had latched onto the story and was running full out on it, prominent attorney murdered, on and on, how Jack Dahlgren had been killed, now Eggerman—their business relationships, their Greenfield childhood. Dahlgren's murder had been slighted in the press. Now they seemed to be making up for it.

Still, the details of the killings, the castrations, the smeared message on the mirror, had been kept from the media. They had backed off their first day coverage, which they had categorized as a ritual killing. The only comment this day was toward the end of the front-page article, "There are rumors, denied by police sources, that the murders involved some sort of bizarre ritual."

Kalinyak and Bobby Mack re-visited the motel where the killing had taken place and the dance joint, Pine Valley. The business of a serious investigation was continuing. A team of police technicians and detectives was in both places, questioning people, taking blood swabs, dusting for prints, measuring distances, collecting room detritus, the dreary nuts and bolts of police work.

They had breakfast at a diner down the road from Pine Valley, then drove toward Tracyville. "Who brought Magpie into this? You said you had a source?"

"One of the hookers from the Hot Box. Said the German had been trying to reach Magpie." He was on the verge of telling Bobby Mack about his daughter, but he just couldn't get it out. He would look for another opportunity.

They learned from the housekeeper that Father Magoczy was in the church. They found him seated on the concrete floor in front of the lectern. A large wooden Christ on the Cross was on the wall in front of him. He was asleep.

Bobby Mack shook him. He opened his bloodshot eyes. "What is it?"

"We have to talk some more, Gussy."

They sat in the church library. Magoczy looked god-awful. He hadn't shaved; his turned-around collar was askew and edged with grime. The housekeeper had come over from the rectory with a pot of coffee. "There's a German girl involved in this," Kalinyak said. "Do you know her?"

"I've seen her," Magoczy said. "She came up here looking for me a while back. I thought she was a ghost."

"Why do you say that?"

"I see things," he said. "When I'm drinking, I see things." He smiled ruefully and shook his head. "Even when I'm not drinking. She came to the house, and when I saw her, I ran. I thought she was a ghost."

"When was this?"

"She came twice. Just before Dahlgren, you know, before he was killed. I saw her and I heard the song. Then she came once again, to the Church."

"Song?" Bobby Mack said.

Magoczy looked at him with a knowing gaze. "The song. The one that was playing."

"What are you talking about?"

"Everyone wants to play dumb. It was her, and then I realized it couldn't be her..."

"What are you talking about?" Kalinyak said. Bobby Mack signaled him to take it easy.

"She was playing some game. Ghost." He looked directly at Bobby Mack. "What do you want to know?"

"Who is this woman? This German woman."

"I don't know."

"Did you talk to her?"

"I told you. I ran away. Both times."

"You never heard her speak?"

"She called out to me. She called me Gus."

"Did she have an accent?"

"How could I tell? 'Gus! Gus!' That's all she said. How did she know my name?"

"You said she came to you twice."

"She came to church once. She stood in the back. She made a signal to me. She called me Gus."

"When was this?"

"I'm not sure. A few days after the first time she showed up."

"The woman who called you to meet Doyle? Was it the same voice?"

"I don't know. I didn't think about it. I thought it was his secretary."

"Did she have an accent?" Kalinyak asked.

"I'm not sure." He remained quiet for a while. "I'm not sure about anything. That's the pity of it all. I do know that we're cursed. Our sins have cast a curse on us. We've all sinned." He made the sign of the cross, while muttering a prayer.

"Oh, Gus," Kalinyak said. "Magpie!" He hugged Magoczy to him.

"I love you, Kalin," the priest said. "You too, Bobby Mack. I love you. I loved the Egg."

"Dahlgren?"

"I hated him."

Kalinyak and Bobby Mack drove back to Pittsburgh in a ferocious thunderstorm. They sat in Bobby Mack's office in the courthouse building and watched the rain streak the window with rivulets of water. Lightning flashed in the distance, thunder growled. "What can it be?" Kalinyak said.

"I've been wracking my brain."

"The two of them messed with the same German hooker? Does that sound right?"

"I don't know," Bobby Mack said. "Where do we go from here?"

"Have to find the German girl..."

"She's probably back in Germany," Bobby Mack said.

"Why do you say that?"

"Would you kill two men and then hang around?"

"Funny how it's all played out," Kalinyak said. "Jack Dahlgren murdered. Doyle. Gus Magoczy, a drunk."

"You lost a daughter."

"Yes. And so did you. In a manner of speaking." He wanted to say something about his old friend's daughter. He couldn't bring himself to talk about it.

"Life is a jack-in-the-box," Bobby Mack said. He reached into his desk and brought out a bottle of whiskey and poured himself a water glass full of the stuff. He sipped at it. Neither of them spoke. The rain lashed the windows. Lightning flashed. Thunder rumbled in the distance.

"I have this emptiness," Kalinyak said.

"I know. I have it, too."

"Who would have thought, back in the old days, Mirror Street Aces, football games, who would thought life could become so harsh and terrible?"

"As kids, we didn't think about those things," Bobby Mack said. "We thought about the next drink, the next girl, the next game. It was all good, then. The world was Mirror Street and Greenfield, and it was all good." He stood up. "I'll drop you at your hotel. It's my night to get laid."

"Theresa?"

"It means nothing to me. It's like a warm piss. It's important to her."

"We'll just have to wait until something breaks," Bobby Mack said on the drive over to the hotel.

"I have this itch," said Kalinyak. "Not so much for Dahlgren, though I did like him more or less. But for Doyle. I have this itch to catch this madwoman."

"Yes," said Bobby Mack.

"And not for today. I hadn't seen Doyle in years. I want to do it for the old days. For what we all were."

"I know, Frankie."

They drove in silence for a while. "What did Jack Dahlgren have to do with the sale of St. Philomena's?" Kalinyak said.

Bobby Mack shook his head. "It was no big thing. Believe me."

At the hotel, Kalinyak paced his room. His daughter's eyes followed him wherever he went. A great welling up of emotion formed somewhere in the center of his chest. He felt that if he began to weep he would never be able to stop.

He called Betty Malloy.

Chapter
Ten

It was after nine p.m. when Kalinyak turned off Fifth Avenue into Squirrel Hill. Betty Malloy's house was North of Forbes, not far from where Eggerman had lived. The street, while not quite as grand as Woodbine, was impressive. A number of great, dark, granite mansions were set back from the tree-shrouded road. The house, up a long brick drive, was stone, covered with ivy.

Kalinyak parked the car and climbed a flight of stone steps to the house. He felt uncomfortable, foolish, out of his league. He rang the bell and waited.

Betty opened the door. She had the old, sweet, quizzical Betty Malloy smile. She looked beautiful, and Kalinyak felt his heart quicken, and he felt stupid, stupid. "Mr. Kalinyak," she said.

"Ms. Malloy." Laughing, she led him into the living room. Large, though not quite as massive as Eggerman's, it exuded a quiet, tasteful sense of wealth. "When Jack and I bought this place, it was *the* house. Doyle was still living off Beechwood, and Jack loved the fact that he had outdone him. By the time Doyle bought the new place, Jack and I were separated. It would have killed him to have seen Doyle living better than him. Doyle had the place on Woodbine? Jack bought homes all over the county. He must have had half a dozen."

"Jack called me once in Arizona years ago," Kalinyak said. "My daughter was still alive. 'I'm sitting in my mansion on Dunridge, looking at my Rolls Corniche in the drive, while my butler serves me brandy. How ya doin', Kalin?' 'I'm doing fine. I'm having a beer. I'm watching my daughter work a jigsaw puzzle.' 'I made over two million dollars last year. How'd you do?' 'Thirty-five thou.' 'You're wasting your life,' he said."

"That's the way he was."

"How did you take it?"

She didn't speak for a moment. She smiled and shrugged. "You know Jack was my first serious boyfriend. And he had a certain really nice side to him, you know the way he was. He always seemed to be enjoying himself. There was never any anger or sadness in his life. I don't know. He acted like he owned you, but then he took very good care of you. I found this—" She picked up a book from a sideboard and brought it to Kalinyak. It was their high school yearbook.

On a large leather couch, they leafed though the book, and Kalinyak was transported back to a time where everything was uncomplicated and fun. There was Frank and Bobby Mack and Doyle and Jack in their football uniforms. There was a very small picture of a girl with freckles, a young girl in the cafeteria.

"Little Miss Personality," Kalinyak said.

"Only picture of me in the book. I was in seventh grade when you were all seniors. Allderdice was goofy, with junior high and high school together. How grown-up we felt when we reached ninth grade."

She turned to the section containing the class graduation pictures, stopping at Kalinyak's picture. He looked very serious, crew cut, suit and tie. "Robert Hall suit," he said. "Dahlgren joked about it. 'Overhead's so low even the mice are hunchbacked.'" Underneath his picture, it said, "Now the parade is almost past. Kalin, our hero, here at last."

"Kalin, our hero! Even then," Betty said.

"Look how pretty she is..." It was Sarah Jo Kaczmarek, her picture right next to Kalinyak's.

"You liked her, didn't you?" Betty Malloy said.

"I liked her. But Jack got to her first. He impressed her with all his money. He always had a big roll of bills. Hustling pool."

"Something happened with her..."

"Went bad. She has a look about her..." Kalinyak was staring at her picture. There was something serious, soulful in her eyes. "It's as though she can see the future," Kalinyak said. "I haven't seen her in all these years. Had even forgotten what she looked like. And yet now, it's as though I had just seen her yesterday." He lapsed into silence. His mind was back in the past.

"What are you thinking about?"

"Oh, we do things in our lives and then we pay for them later. She had a tough time of it. I had my tragedy. And now Jack and Doyle. We never could have imagined it back then. The directions our lives would go in. This thing with Jack and Doyle. It's a terrible, terrible thing. I somehow think that unless I take care of it, no one's going to take care of it."

"You were the one who had to take care of everything."

"I felt responsible."

They kissed. It was soft and gentle, without passion, a kiss between a brother and sister. "That's funny," she said.

"What?"

"I don't know."

He felt awkward and stupid, and she saw it and began to laugh. "What?" he said.

"You're just very funny. You always were. You always could make me laugh. So. What do you think?"

"About what?"

"That we could— after all these years?"

He didn't speak for a long time. He toyed with her hair. "I'm empty, you know. I have nothing to give to anybody."

"That's a stupid thing to say," she said.

"You're the best. I'm—" He struggled with the words.

"What?"

"Empty."

"Why do you say that?"

"Dead inside."

"No," she said. "You've gone through certain things. That's what it is. I understand that." She got up. "What can I get for you? I know you don't drink. Soft drink?"

"That would be good."

She left the room, and he walked to a wall covered with bookcases. There were a number of framed photographs of her and Dahlgren and their kids. Dahlgren was astonishingly handsome in those days. He thought of the death photograph of him he had seen in Bobby Mack's office and he shuddered. "Ah, Jack. Jack," he said quietly.

Betty returned with a tray. On it were two glasses filled with Coca-Cola and a plate of finger sandwiches. "These were left over from the other evening at Eggerman's. They might be a little stale."

"I don't know what to do about this thing," he said. "These killings. We're at a dead-end."

"The paper said something about a prostitute."

"Yes. A woman. A pro. Jack had something with her. Foreign girl, German or something."

"Prostitute. That would be Jack's style, but what would it have to do with Doyle?"

"They were in business together."

"They did a lot of business together. Jack burned Doyle more than once. Doyle always shrugged it off. 'When you deal with the devil,' he used to say, 'don't be surprised when everything goes to hell.' He knew what he was doing."

"This prostitute is very elusive. Has a reputation for being a loner. Maybe psychotic. Bobby Mack's daughter knows her."

"His daughter? Lisa?"

"She calls herself Lara."

"It's Lisa. I was at her baptism. How did you come to her?"

"She's a hooker."

"Oh, my God."

"Works out of a bar on Smithfield."

"I know that his daughter had problems. Does Bobby know that you're—"

"No."

"You have to tell him."

"I know. It's tough for me."

"I understand. But you have to tell him. Oh, my God..."

"Jack gets involved with this girl, this German girl, this pro. Beats her up."

"That's possible."

"She's crazy. She decides to off him. Why does she go after Doyle? Did he mess around?"

"Never. Mr. Straight Arrow."

"So how does he get involved with this crazy?"

"Why are you doing this?" she asked.

"What do you mean?"

"You come from Arizona and you're working on this— case. Why?"

"Bobby asked me to help. I mean, Jack was a close friend of mine. Doyle. We were all very close. You know this." He sipped at his Coca-Cola. He realized Betty was staring at him with a watchfulness that was unsettling. He sensed she pitied him and he felt clumsy beyond measure, stupid, lost.

"How was your life in Arizona?"

He didn't speak for a long time. "After my daughter's death, I had no life."

"I understand."

"That's the truth of it."

She put her hand on his shoulder and massaged it. "You're such a good man."

"No. I'm really not. I've done some terrible things."

"I doubt it."

"Well." He drained his glass and stood. "I have to take care of some things."

"I'm glad you've come back. If you need anything."

"I appreciate that."

"You're kind of at a dead end."

"I am. Yes."

"We'll fix it up." She smiled. Her smile was glorious. "I like you a lot," she said.

"I like you, too."

She winked at him, a slow wink, and he realized they used to do that as kids, all of them. It had been some kind of ritual. Had they borrowed it from a film? He winked back. She shook her head, still smiling. "It'll all work out," she said.

He drove to the area near his hotel and parked in front of the Aida. It was after midnight. Inside, he asked for Cory. The bartender shook his head. "I think he's gone," he said.

"Think he might be at The Strip?"

"I mean gone. You hear things, you know? I think all the cops spooked him. Everyone's spooked."

He drove to the Hot Box. Lara was there with several girl friends. Two heavy-set men sat at a corner table, obviously cops. "What's become of Cory?" he asked her. Her pupils were pinned.

"He's gone with the wind," she said.

"Make a good title for a movie."

"If that's the best you can do, cowboy, get out of Dodge."

* * *

The investigation settled into something routine, plodding. Cops canvassed all the downtown and strip bars, hangouts, dance halls. They were painstakingly piecing together bits and pieces of information. "None of it amounts to diddly-squat," Bobby Mack told Kalinyak.

Kalinyak, for his part, spent every waking hour in the Strip area at the Hot Box, the Aida Lounge, talking to people, prodding them, trying to intimidate or charm them, hookers, hustlers, pimps, junkies, the snake belly of late night Pittsburgh.

A week went by. There were no leads. Everything had dried up.

A deep sense of frustration, of defeat, had come over Kalinyak. He had trouble sleeping, and when he would finally drift off, he'd have ugly dreams. He would dream of the old days, high school days, grammar school, Jack Dahlgren and Doyle Eggerman. He would dream of St. Philomena's, the ball field, the coal mine, Dahlgren stashing his burglary swag in the pond in front of the church and in the old coal mine. He would dream of confessing his sins to Father Stan.

In one dream, he had pulled the plywood barrier away from the entrance to the coal mine. He was with Gus Magoczy, and they were both teenagers. They were walking along the coal mine shaft corridor. He could see the rusted coal car tracks snaking along the shaft and smell the dark, moldy odor of the mine.

There was a loud sound of water dripping somewhere down the shaft corridor. He had a flashlight, and he shined it on the black coal walls of the mine. His nostrils stung with coal dust.

And then he saw a girl. She was young, also a teenager, and quite pretty. Her startlingly blue eyes were wide with terror. She was nailed on a cross of mine timbers. Blood was dripping from where the nails had penetrated her hands; it was the sound they had heard upon entering the mine.

The girl was his daughter.

"Dear God," he heard himself say aloud. She was not the age she had been when she was killed, but as she might have been had she grown to be a teenager. "It's St. Philomena," Magoczy said in a hushed voice. He dipped his hands in her blood and touched them to his head and made the sign of the cross and began to pray. "St. Philomena, faithful imitator of Mary..."

Kalinyak awoke feeling ill. His mouth was dry. He had a vague headache.

He had coffee in the hotel room and then hurried outside. The day was humid, the sky dark, rain on its way, a thunder storm approaching.

It was a ten-minute walk down Liberty Avenue to the Boulevard of the Allies and the *Pittsburgh Post-Gazette* building. His shirt was soaked with perspiration. There was a low rumble of thunder in the distance.

He showed his DA credentials at the reception desk and was directed to an elevator that took him to the basement and a large file area. Again, he had to present his credentials. A stooped man at a metal desk took him back into a series of corridors lined with file cabinets. "If it happened before 1993, it won't be on our computers," the man said. He sat Kalinyak down at a table with a microfilm projector and brought him several reels of film.

Though there were a number of articles about the sale of St. Philomena's, everything seemed vague to Kalinyak, confused: everyone interviewed seemed to be avoiding something. The chief financial officer of the Catholic Diocese of Pittsburgh, a man by the name of Harrington, questioned about the sale, spoke of the shifting Catholic demographics in Pittsburgh. "We have problems. A shrinking income base. I have to deal with the fiscal affairs of a $20 million organization— 700 full and part-time employees."

The head of the Diosese, Bishop Daniel Zalimicros, was equally fuzzy about the sale. The church, he insisted, was not concerned about making money, but it did need to balance its budget. "We are a church prepared for the new millennium. The Diocese is facing challenges. Fewer priests, fewer parishioners, more costs for technology and staffing. Unlike most businesses, the church gets most of its money from offertory revenue, people donating money. Rather than following modern commercial codes, its financial doctrine is governed by centuries-old canon law." He was pressed on the deal for St. Philomena's. "We didn't gain from it," he said. "This was all the Redemptorists in New York. A Catholic missionary society. They owned the land. We owned nothing." The interview had taken place in the main church of the diocese, St. Paul's Cathedral in Oakland.

It was pouring rain when Kalinyak left the Post-Gazette building. Rather than walk back to the hotel, he hailed a cab on Liberty Avenue and took it up the Boulevard of the Allies. "You know St. Paul's Cathedral in Oakland?"

"The church or the parish offices? The church is on Fifth Avenue, the offices around the corner on Dithridge Street."

"The offices."

The church was a large, gothic-style structure not far from the University of Pittsburgh's Cathedral of Learning. Behind the church was a small building, which housed the parish offices. Kalinyak explained to a receptionist why he was there. She excused herself and moved briskly into a back office. She returned a moment later and escorted him into the office.

The rector of the church, Father Birghulce, was stocky and balding, in his sixties, with skin smooth and pink as a baby's. He made no effort to conceal his lack of interest in Kalinyak and his visit. "Yes, St. Philomena's. There was some controversy. To be frank with you, I don't know much about it. It was a deal structured by the Redemptorists. You would have to talk to them, or the people from the Jewish Educational Alliance who bought the church." He was working on a schedule of sorts, a poster-board chart, and went immediately back to it.

Kalinyak thanked him. Father Birghulce forced a smile. As Kalinyak reached the door to the office, he heard the priest say very softly, "What does this have to do with those murdered men?"

Kalinyak turned. The priest's gray eyes were flat and dull. "Nothing," Kalinyak said. "As far as I know nothing."

The priest stared at him and did not blink.

Kalinyak hurried from the parish offices. He took yet another cab into Squirrel Hill. The rain was falling in great sheets, flooding the streets. Thunder cracked and continuous flashes of lightning lit up the sky. "You know St. Philomena's, where it used to be? Beechwood, not far from Allderdice?"

"It's a Jew place now, right?" the cabbie said, a small, gnomish man who spoke with an accent. "I have nothing against the Jews. I'm a Jew myself. Odessa. Ever hear of that place? Part of Soviet Union, now is Ukraine. I'm from Moldvanka neighborhood, Jew ghetto, Squirrel Hill of Odessa."

He pulled up a long asphalt drive to the front of the building. The pond was still there, lilies covering the surface of the water. Rain splattered the lilies.

Kalinyak could see no indication that this granite structure had once been a church. The stone crosses and religious statuettes had all been removed, angels and saints, Fathers of the Church. There was a large blue Jewish star in a window above the great wooden front doors.

Inside the building, nothing seemed familiar to him. He was in the school section of the building, but it had been completely renovated and he recognized nothing except the bleak, gray slate that formed the floor. There was a sign on a door, "Mitchell Kotkin, Administrator."

A secretary took him into the administrator's office. Kalinyak estimated that Kotkin was near his age, perhaps forty-five, heavy-set, balding, an ex-athlete gone to seed. "I hope I'm not disturbing you," Kalinyak said, presenting his ID.

"DA's office. Special Investigator?"

"I'm interested in the sale of St. Philomena's. You've heard of these murders...?"

"Dahlgren and Eggerman?"

"Yes."

"I've been following the whole thing. Tragic. Bizarre. I knew them both...From way back. Allderdice."

"I thought you looked familiar..."

"You are—?"

"Frank Kalinyak."

"Of course! When I saw your ID, rang a bell— The Hunky Hurricane... Mirror Street Aces. The Huns!"

"The Huns, yes."

"I was a Tartar. Mirror Street Aces, you had some good, tough players. Bobby Mack, Dahlgren."

"The Tartars were good. We had some games..."

"There was a game we played, baseball, you guys, at the field at the bottom of Greenfield Avenue—"

"That's right..."

"And we were beating you and suddenly fights started breaking out all over the field?"

"I do remember that."

"I went running up to you to see if you could control your guys and you punched me in the mouth." Mitchell Kotkin laughed.

"Well, in those days," Kalinyak said, "you know, mixing the Huns and the Tartars was like oil and water, the hunkies and the Jews. That was like oil and water."

"It was."

"I apologize for what I did that day. I'm sorry for a lot of things we did in those days."

They both grew quiet. "You put on some weight," Kalinyak said after a while.

Mitchell Kotkin laughed. "In those days, I looked like Marlon Brando when he was young and sleek. And when I got older I still looked like him, a fat tub. How can I help you, Frank?"

"What happened in that sale?"

"What do you mean?"

"I know it wasn't popular. And I can't seem to get any solid information about what went on. Even the Diocese doesn't want to talk about it. What happened?"

Kotkin shook his head. "Oh, very complicated. A lot of skids to grease."

"Even with the church?"

"You have to understand, the Pittsburgh diocese had nothing to do with it. The Redemptorists in Brooklyn just wanted out. A deal was brokered." He winked knowingly. "So—"

"So?"

"The Huns—"

"The Huns?"

"Dahlgren, Eggerman, Bobby Mack—"

"Brokered it?"

"Made a nice bit of change. It was all done behind the scenes, smoke and mirrors. You know there was a lot of anger over this thing. Some anti-Jewish feeling even."

"Would someone kill over it?"

Mitchell Kotkin shook his head and stared directly at Kalinyak. "Why would they?" he said. "What else can I do for you, Frank?"

"What's become of the old coal mine?"

"Oh, that's been barricaded for years..."

"It's still here?"

"Oh, yes. The church used it for storage. Yes, it's still here."

"Storage?"

"Junk mainly."

"Could I look at it?"

"Nothing much there. Dank. Coal dust. Some junk left there from years back. Why are you interested?"

"You know, I went to St. Philomena's, the grade school. We used to play in the mine, sneak in there."

"You know the church heated their buildings with coal from the mine for years."

"I know."

"And who knows. Maybe one day we'll do it again. Though I think the mine is pretty well depleted."

"Was it just coal there?"

"What do you mean? Was there also gold or uranium? No, just coal, and not a very good grade at that. We considered filling the mine with concrete. We decided it wasn't worth the effort or the expense. That mine goes back quite a distance."

Kotkin called to his secretary. "Have Hirsch take Mr. Kalinyak into the mine..."

The mine was just below the ball field, up the drive from the main building. The outer entrance was inaccessible, completely walled up. There was a door, however, leading from the basement of the administration building into the mine. Hirsch, an elderly man in shiny dark trousers and a gray sweater, opened the large metal door and brought Kalinyak into the mine-shaft. "There's some lighting in this area. I wouldn't go too deep." He threw a switch and a line of dull, yellowish lights came on. "I'll wait for you here."

Kalinyak moved down the shaft. It was as he remembered it and as it was in his dream, black coal walls, rusted mine car tracks. The air was dank, moist, oppressive. He listened for a dripping sound. He could only hear a quiet hum from the metal lighting fixtures conduit.

He moved a hundred feet or so into the shaft. He came to a wider area, a chamber where the coal had been removed. The line of lights ended here. There was a rusted metal car where the tracks also ended.

Piled against one wall were school desks, chairs, tattered books, plaster of paris religious statuettes, pictures, carvings, rugs. He approached the junk pile. He wondered if any of Jack Dahlgren's swag was still there.

He found some torn photographs of grade school classes. He recognized several of the nuns in the pictures as well as Father Stan. He didn't recognize any of the students. There was a large carton labeled, "St. Philomena Parish Annual Reports".

He opened the carton. There were stacks of file folders filled with typed reports and dates going back to the forties. He could make no sense of them.

He found a primitive carving of a woman. Above it was written, Our Mother of Perpetual Help. And next to that, printed in block letters: "Mary's mouth is small, she speaks little."

He felt oppressed by the dank air, the yellowish light, the low hum from the electrical conduit. Why had he come here?

He heard a sound behind him. It was the old man, Hirsch, moving awkwardly toward him down the corridor. He looked like a ghost in the dull light. He was perspiring. "Some stuff," the old man said. "I keep telling them, they should have a yard sale up on where the ball field used to be. Probably some very sentimental stuff there. But the powers that be don't want to stir up old feelings. When you release old feelings, they tell me, you never know what might come to the surface..."

"I've seen enough," Kalinyak said, suddenly desperately tired, forlorn. He hurried back up the shaft toward the iron door and the building basement. He could hear the old man struggling to keep up with him.

* * *

"I have to find this guy Cory. Work him," Kalinyak said to Bobby Mack as they had breakfast at Johnny McGuire's. "Where could he have gone?" He was buttering a side order of rye toast. It was as though he were talking to himself.

"How're you going to find him?"

"There's this hooker. I think she'll be able to help me."

"Okay."

They didn't talk for a while. Finally, Kalinyak said, "I didn't know that you, Dahlgren, and Eggerman were in on the St. Philomena's deal."

Bobby had a water glass of scotch in front of him. He held it up and swished the liquor around, then took a long swallow. He stared at Kalinyak and it was not comfortable look. "What brought this up?" Kalinyak remained silent. "What are you trying to do?"

"Do? Nothing. I just feel like I'm in the middle of—I don't know— You and Dahlgren and Eggerman are involved here, in this thing, and now there's the killings, Egg and Dahlgren. And I have no idea what—what's going on. Is there an okay-doke here? Maybe someone in that whole thing thought they were being cheated or something."

"Just wait a second, Frankie. Don't get on your high horse here. What whole thing?" Bobby Mack had raised his voice. His face was flushed.

"This St. Philomena's deal."

"I made a few bucks. Is that all right?"

"It's all right, Bobby."

"The church was being sold, it had to be sold, and I was only a participant in helping the deal go through."

"Greasing the skids?"

"In a manner of speaking."

"How much force was exerted to get the deal through?"

"What's that supposed to mean?"

"Well, you're from the D.A.'s office. There was a reason why you were brought into the thing." Bobby Mack sat there, his face flushed with anger, his expression bleak. "You just should have told me."

"It was nothing I feel proud about. Okay? It was Dahlgren who brought me in. I been working for Allegheny County over twenty years. What do I have? A house on Anita Street? A pot to piss in, don't even have that. Yes, Dahlgren asks me to grease some skids. I did it. I made out real good. We all did. That's the alpha and omega of the whole thing. No okay-doke."

"All right."

"The church in New York—"

"The Redemptorists?"

"Congregation of the Most Holy Redeemer. Missionary society. Catholic missionaries. They're perfection, for chrissake. I was dealing with saints, holy folk grateful for their Mission in the Church, grateful to announce the Mystery of the Word, grateful to illuminate the mystery of humanity. In dealing with them, this is what I had to listen to. Mystery within mystery, all this church bullshit." Bobby Mack held his glass of scotch up high, as though in a toast. His eyes were watery from the booze. "The love of God made visible in Jesus Christ embraces everyone, witness to the truth that whoever follows Christ, the perfect human being, becomes more human."

"Okay."

Bobby Mack drained the glass. "All bullshit, we know this. We been to Catholic school, had the nuns rap our knuckles, Father Ignatius grab our pecker, etcetera." He laughed loudly, signaled to the waiter to refill his glass. "The Redemptorists, they owned the land, owned St. Phil's, wanted out. They were savvy, these saints. They could see the handwriting on the wall. When poor St. Philomena was stamped null and void by Rome, a lot of the parish jumped ship, went to Bethel Park, St. Bonaventure in Glenshaw, St. Casimir. Scattered. Losing proposition. The Pittsburgh

Diocese owned none of St. Phil's land, the coal mine, church, school, yet they footed the bill. Everyone said dump it."

"Where'd Dahlgren come in?"

"Where does Dahlgren ever come in? Front door, back door, side door. There were about three hundred churchgoers that were against any sale. These were old-timers, politico powerhouses. Brendan Macha, those people. Suddenly everyone backed off. Here was this prime bit of real estate, Squirrel Hill, Beechwood Boulevard, and no one will buy. So Doyle and Jackie set it up with the Jews. All under the table, behind the scenes. Oh, what an uproar that caused! So I was the liaison between Macha and Doyle and Jackie. The Jews paid top dollar. Dahlgren and Doyle and me split a nice fee. What you would call a finders fee. Macha got his, you can be sure. And that's the long and the short of it."

"Nice."

"We were brokers, brokered money, but really a pay-off. What the Jews called 'a shmear.' St. Phil's meant a lot to a lot of people, you know this. We seriously pissed off a number of people, for the almighty dollar."

"What were the legalities?"

"It was legal, but was it moral? In the middle of the night, that's what I ask myself. It might have been legal, but was it moral?"

"Business is business. When has morality ever trumped business?"

"That's what I tell myself. When we were young, Dahlgren screwed me on some business thing. I said, 'Jack, how could you do that to me, your friend.' 'Hey, Bobby,' he says, 'Friendship is one thing, but business is business.' "

"That's the way of the world," Kalinyak said. Again, they lapsed into silence. Bobby Mack ordered another drink. Kalinyak stirred milk into his coffee. At last he said, "There's this problem that I was telling you about, with Cory and this hooker."

"What?"

"The hooker."

"What about her? What?"

Kalinyak took in a deep breath. "Your daughter."

There was a long silence. Bobby Mack suddenly looked older than his forty-eight years. He slumped forward. His voice was hoarse. "What does she have to do with this?"

"She was friends with both the guy and the German girl."

"Why didn't you tell me?"

"It was uncomfortable for me."

Bobby Mack had grown very serious, which was something unusual for him. Kalinyak had always loved Bobby Mack because, above all things, he was never serious. You always knew that when you were in Bobby Mack's presence, you were going to have a good time.

"Do what you have to do," Bobby Mack said.

"It's tough," Kalinyak said.

"Yeah." Bobby Mack exhaled.

"I'm sorry."

"This kid has been a knife in my heart, Frank. When she was young, she was everything to me. Well, you know how that is."

"Yes."

"And when she started to go bad, I tried everything. It was her mother, her mother's influence. Her life style. She was a glorified whore. What chance did the kid have? I tried, Kalin. Nothing worked. A knife in my heart. Look after her, if you can."

"Why don't you talk to her?"

"I come into a place, restaurant, any place, she sees me, she runs away. She blames me."

"For what?"

"Not fighting her mother. Not going to bat for her. She accuses me. It's all my fault. How important is she to all of this?"

"In any obvious way, not important at all. On the periphery. But maybe she knows something, one little thing. I don't know. I have to work this guy, Cory. It's all I have."

"Don't get her into trouble." Kalinyak held up his hand as if to say, don't even mention it.

"This fucking life," Bobby Mack said with sudden fury.

"You gotta be strong, Bobby. We all know this."

"But how much can we take? How much? It's like we're cursed." He stared at Kalinyak a long time. He knows something, Kalinyak was thinking. Something, too, was bubbling underneath, bubbling in Kalinyak's consciousness. Something here, he found himself thinking. Some knot here. What? What curse had seized them all with its malevolent power?

Chapter Eleven

Kalinyak returned to the Aida yet another time. Another week had gone by. Kalinyak had walked the downtown streets. Crossed and re-crossed the bridges. Took his car all over the old Hill District. Visited every late night joint, tavern, diner, club within a twenty-mile radius of the downtown area.

He had driven out to Pine Valley, sat and watched the dancers on the small dance floor. Strolled among the motels.

He felt like some late night creep, a vampire on the prowl.

The leaves on the trees were changing color now, falling. Living in Arizona, he hadn't experienced this in years, and he found it unsettling. He had always found it depressing, the autumnal changing of color. The world was dying, it seemed to say. The sky would become heavy and gray, and there would be a sharp bite in the air, and winter would be not far off.

"He hasn't been here. I told you," the bartender said. "You never going to find him. He's spooked. I could tell."

"Where's he from?"

"Upstate somewhere."

"Where?"

"Maybe Oil City, up around there."

"Why do you say that?"

"I just always associated Oil City with him."

"What's his last name?"

"Damned if I know."

Kalinyak left the Aida and walked over to the Hot Box. The neon sign was dark. It was shut down tight, with a sign on the door that said, "CLOSED UNTIL FURTHER NOTICE."

He drove into the Strip District and entered the Hard Luck Café. The heavy police presence had affected business there, also. It was graveyard quiet. A few young people in punk make-up lounged in a corner of the place. "Do you know Cory?" Kalinyak asked the bartender, a man with tattoos and a stainless steel stud in his lower lip.

"Jesus, another one? All we get these days is overweight middle-age guys who sweat too much asking about this person and that person. Yeah, I know Cory. What about him?"

"Have you seen him?"

"Not for more than a week."

"What's his last name? Where does he live?"

"Have no fucking idea."

"The German girl?"

"The squeeze? Damn, everyone's looking for her. If I knew where she was, I'd be a big hero."

Kalinyak noticed Lara seated by herself in shadow at a table by the exit door. She looked sullen, angry. "What's the matter?"

"*Filoriandro...*"

"Filor—?"

She mimed putting a needle in her arm. "That's what the spics say; you know my friend, Tina, little Puerto Rican, that's what she says. *Filoriandro*. Ah, this life..."

"Strung out?"

She laughed bitterly. "Always strung out unless I'm high and I don't look high now, do I? That's a given."

"What's your problem?"

"My father's been asking for me. Going around with the cops. Cops been asking for me. Jesus."

"What's Cory's name, you know, his whole name?"

"Fuck Cory!"

"I need to find him. Where does he live?"

"Have no fucking idea."

"Where's he from originally?"

"Up north somewhere."

"Oil City?"

"Sounds right."

"What's his full name?"

"Went by the name of Devereaux, but that wasn't his real name. Delos is what his driver's license says."

"Cory Delos?"

"Steven Delos."

"Jesus. Okay. Good. If I see your father, you want me to give him a message?"

"Yeah. Tell him to go fuck himself."

"Nice."

"That's the way it is." She raised her middle finger to Kalinyak and shoved it into the air.

"Very nice."

"I should give a shit..."

"Okay. Take care."

"I'll take it any way I can get it, sport."

"Sport?"

She smiled grimly. "You're a player, aren't you?"

"Lisa, take it easy, okay?"

"How'd you know my name? My father?"

"Betty Malloy."

"Asshole Jack Dahlgren's wife?"

"Yes."

"Happiest day in the Burg is when they offed Jack Dahlgren."

"You hated him."

"Beat the living shit out of me."

"I know this. Put you in the hospital. Others?"

"A ton."

"Boys or girls?"

She laughed. "You know Asshole Jack would never pick on a boy... Psycho motherfucker. You say hello to Betty. She's good people. How she ended up with Dahlgren is one of the great mysteries of the world. Hey, if you're looking for people who wanted Jack Dahlgren dead, the line starts around the block..."

Kalinyak walked over to the courthouse building. A sharp wind whipped down Smithfield, chasing scraps of paper and leaves before it. Inside Bobby Mack's office, he and Hanratty were polishing off a bottle. "Mayor's having a shit fit," Hanratty said. "Save us, Kalin, save us." His face was flushed and he was perspiring.

"I'm doing my best."

"Not good enough! Greenfield here give me your expense statement. Damn, you're pricey."

"Deal like this, you got to pass around the sugar."

"I was kidding. You're cheap at twice the ticket."

"There's not enough cabbage in the world to pay Kalin what he's really worth," Bobby Mack said, voice thick, eyes teary from booze. "You're the man, Frank. Always were, always will be. Frankie on the Spot! This guy, Phil? You're in the red zone, need six points, give Kalin the ball. You're all the way back, back to goal-line, desperate to get out, give Kalin the ball. He'll get you ninety-nine yards. This is the man."

"I always heard that about you, Frank," Hanratty said.

"I'm going to take a drive up to Oil City," Kalinyak said.

"What the fuck for?"

"I got a lead on this kid, this Cory. He might be hiding out up there. The German girl—"

"This Marika whatever her name is?" Hanratty said. He reached across Bobby Mack and lifted the bottle, Glenlivet scotch, from the table. Poured a water glass full of the stuff.

"This Cory and this Marika, there's something there."

"Should have brought the fucker in two weeks ago," Bobby Mack said. "Beat the living shit out of him. We'd know where Miss Marika is..."

Hanratty laughed. "Hey, Bobby, Bobby—we don't do things that way any more. You know that."

"The old ways were the best ways. We never had to fuck around like we're doing here. Get you a hot lead and third degree him until he coughs up every-fucking-thing."

"That's the old way," Hanratty said.

"Fucking-A. And can you tell me a better way? You get up to Oil City, Kalin. Or wherever the fuck. And you find this Cory. And you third-degree the motherfucker. You squeeze his balls until he hollers uncle, aunt, and all the cousins. Let's wrap this motherfucker! Let's clean this up! Hey, Phil, they fucked with the Huns! Did you know that Kalin and me and Jack Dahlgren and the Egg--we were all Huns."

"You've told me this."

"This was over on Mirror Street. Fucking Mirror Street. You'd think with a name like that, you could hold the street up to your face and see what the hell you were about. Not Mirror Street. Should have called it Smoke and Mirror Street. You know this, Kalin, don't deny it. We did things." He put his finger up to his lips. "Mum's the word." He smiled.

"Yeah. Okay. So you're giving me the office to third-degree the guy?"

"Damn straight—"

"Wait one second. No, you don't do that," Hanratty said. "You Mirandize the guy. That's what you do."

"Bull-fucking-shit!" Bobby Mack yelled. "Mirandize my asshole. Frankie's not official. He's a hired gun. Kalin, you third-degree him."

Hanratty made a sign to Frank, as if to say, don't listen to him; he's had too much to drink.

"I'm off," Kalinyak said.

"Did you see my daughter?" Bobby Mack said, suddenly quiet, sober.

"Briefly. She's—all right."

"Yeah. Okay. All right. You take care"

"You, too."

Bobby Mack stared at his glass. "I love you, Kalin," he said at last.

"I love you, too, Bobby."

"What do we got here? A couple of quiffs? Petticoats showing?" Hanratty said, laughing loudly.

Bobby grabbed him in a headlock. "I'll give you quiff. How's this for quiff?" He twisted Hanratty's head. "Here's your petticoat!"

"Uncle! Uncle!" Hanratty yelled.

"That's his problem," Bobby Mack said. "Always yelling uncle."

"Hey, Frankie—don't be hiring a Lear Jet to get to Oil City. It's only an hour, hour and a half up the road."

"You have an Oil City phone book?"

Hanratty waved to a book case. There was a shelf of Pennsylvania, West Virginia, and Ohio phone books. "What're you looking for?" Bobby said.

"See if there's a phone for this guy..." He looked up Delos. Not one in the book. "Of course. It would never be that easy..."

The days were getting shorter. There was a chill in the air. He was no sooner out of the city than evening came down. He followed a four-lane part of the way and then cut over to a two-lane, which angled northeast, a shortcut to Oil City.

The countryside was bleak in the thick evening light. The trees were shedding their leaves. He came to the town, moved along Main Street above the Allegheny River. He drove past factories, freight yards, an oil well supply company. Everything appeared dark, rusted. Shuttered, brick buildings lined the street. It all seemed closed down, deserted, and Kalinyak felt uncomfortable in his skin. Why am I here, he found himself asking aloud? Where do I begin?

It had begun to rain. Heavy, thick drops splattered his windshield. The river was dark, viscous, an oily sheen on its surface. Of course, Kalinyak thought: Oil City.

A diner near the freight yard was open. He entered and sat at the counter. He ordered a cup of split pea soup and a bacon, lettuce, and tomato sandwich. The counterman was pudgy with deep-set eyes. "I'm looking for Delos. Do you know anyone by that name?"

"Not around here. Someone works here, you mean?"

"Someone who lives here. Steve Delos."

He shook his head and went back to wiping down a stainless steel area behind the counter.. The place smelled of grease and bug spray, and Kalinyak was sorry he had ordered anything. The counterman brought him his food, but he had lost his appetite. He tasted the soup and took several bites of the sandwich and pushed it to one side. He exited the diner.

He walked down the street aimlessly. It was raining, but not heavily, thick drops that splattered the sidewalk in a nondescript pattern.

The air had a pungent odor as though something was burning, tires perhaps. The street was deserted. He turned up Petroleum Street and came to a suspension bridge and crossed the bridge.

He saw lights from a row of stores, and he walked in that direction. It was an area of workingclass taverns. He entered the first one he came to, The Oil Derrick. It was dark and drab. A half-dozen workmen sat at the bar watching television above the counter. Another handful of men sat at tables. A hockey game was on the television, the Johnstown Chiefs against the Dayton Bombers. The transmission was crude, a local cable system.

Kalinyak ordered a beer and asked the bartender if he knew a Steve Delos. The bartender shook his head. "What do you want with him?"

"Just looking for him."

"Anybody know a Delos?" the bartender said.

"Steve Delos," Kalinyak said.

"Delos. Delos. Weird Steve," a heavyset man at the end of the bar said. "Yeah, I knew him. Went to Central Avenue School with him."

"Were can I find him?"

"Damned if I know. That was more than ten years ago. He left town. He was a weird one, you know."

"What do you mean?"

"Had no real friends. Just a loner. Lived with his mom above Relief Street. Shack way up the hill there. He always had big ideas. He was going to do this, he was going to do that. Alls I know he ever did was get the shit kicked out of him."

The men at the bar laughed. "Common occurrence," one of the men said. "Hummingbird ass weren't as big as his alligator mouth..."

"Where's Relief Street?"

"Go back across this bridge here. That's the Petroleum Street Bridge. You'll cross the railroad tracks. Turn right through the freight yard there and then you'll come to Relief Street, short street between the tracks and the river. Follow it up the hill. No longer a street, just a path. Shack is up there, I don't know, partway up the hill. Lot of junk up there. Used to be a whorehouse up there. When we were kids. That was the problem there with Stevie Delos. His mom was a whore. Don't know if she's still around or not."

Kalinyak went back to his car, drove it across the bridge. The rain had increased. He found Relief Street and drove away from the river partway up the hill. The street ended. The path was asphalt and it continued up through a thicket of trees and weeds. Junk—old tires, crates, automobile parts—was scattered on both sides of the path.

He got out of the car and started up the path. It was very dark out. The asphalt ended. A network of rivulets swirled about his feet. He was tramping through mud. The hill leveled off and he could see a shack ahead of him, clapboard and tar-paper. It was dark. He moved close to the shack.

There was a small yard and a chain link fence. He heard a low growl and a sound of chain unraveling, a rapid rustling sound; a dark form rushed the fence and then an eruption of furious barking. The dog, a huge mastiff, hit the fence then fell backward. On a long chain, it snarled and barked and fought to get free.

Though the shack remained dark, Kalinyak had a feeling that someone was watching him. He sensed something moving behind a black window. He considered calling out, but the mastiff's wild snarls and ferocious barks militated against it. A beast like this, he told himself: be lucky if only a shotgun was backing it up. He weighed the possibilities and concluded it would be better to return the next day when it was light out.

He trekked back down to his car. The dog continued snarling and barking. It began to howl, long, eerie, painful.

He drove back down the hill. At the bottom, he turned left on Main Street. It was not yet eight; he called Magpie on his cell phone. The priest sounded tired, but sober. "It's Kalin. I'm in Oil City. I was thinking about paying you a visit."

"I'd like that. I was just on my way out—"

"Where?"

"I'm restless."

"Nightcap?"

"I have a tough time sleeping. I get nightmares. I pray. It doesn't help. You're not too far. We could meet. We could talk, Frank. I want to talk to you."

"All right."

"Café Russniaki. Same place we met before. You know where?"

"I'll find it."

"Corner of Fifth Street and Eighth Avenue."

It rained the distance to Tracyville, sometimes hard. He crossed the river into town. Beneath the iron bridge, the water appeared swollen and angry under the yellow bridge lights.

Magpie, looking pale and tense, an unhealthy sag to his face, was sitting at the same table as when Kalinyak was last there. He had a single beer in front of him. "I'm trying to cut back," he said as Kalinyak joined him.

Lud, the owner came to the table and Kalinyak ordered a Coca-Cola. "We got the *ledvinky* again."

"The fried kidneys you had last time," Magoczy said.

"I enjoyed them."

"Enjoyed that piss taste, huh," Lud said, laughing.

"They were excellent. I'm not hungry. I was just over in Oil City. Had a BLT."

"How's everything in Oil City?" Lud said.

"I imagine the way it's always been."

"That's true of this whole area. This whole area's been dying ever since I was born." He moved off. Magpie lit a cigarette, offered one to Kalinyak. Kalinyak shook his head, no.

"You don't indulge in nothing, do you?" the priest said. "That's good. You're better off. I'm trying to cut back on my vices."

"When this German girl came to see you—what happened exactly?"

The priest thought for a long time. He stared at Kalinyak through thick, rimless spectacles. "A car pulled up in front of the house. A man was driving. I saw him from the parlor window. The car just sat there for a long time. I could see it under the street light. Then a while later—I was in the back—the doorbell rang. Mrs. Duvka, the housekeeper, she answered, said there was a woman to see me. The woman was right behind her. Blonde woman. There was something about her—she frightened me. I heard—"

"What?"

"Song."

"Song?"

"In my head...I yelled to her to leave, I didn't want to have anything to do with her. She called me Gus. I said Dahlgren has something to do with this."

"Why Dahlgren?"

"I have these dreams. I thought this was a dream. I began to yell; sometimes when I'm drinking I see things. Sometimes I yell. Behave badly. The woman ran off. Later, I looked out the window. The car was still there. It drove off slowly."

"And the time at the church?"

"A Sunday morning, I'm sure. I was speaking that morning. Sometimes I speak, not often. Sometimes. The man came in first. I didn't recognize him. He left. Then I looked up and she was standing at the back of the church. She was moving her mouth. Gus, she was saying. She was shaking her head. She looked hurt. Then she was gone."

"Are you sure someone was there?"

"No. I'm not sure."

"You mentioned a song. What song?"

He shook his head for a very long time. Hummed something. "Don't you remember?"

"What?"

"Dahlgren?"

"I remember Dahlgren. What about him?"

"He cursed us. It started with him."

"Gus, what started with him?"

"We were good boys, all of us. He was the devil. You didn't realize this. He forced me, you know."

"What are you talking about?"

"You know. When the woman called, I knew who it was. I was going down there because I knew who it was. He led us into temptation, he delivered us to evil...I'm weak, Kalin. I'm so weak...I'm out of touch..."

"Out of touch with what?"

"Out of touch." He reached into his pocket and took out a folded sheet of paper. It was a picture cut from a magazine. It was a blonde girl, a movie starlet, a German. She was nude. She looked vaguely like the German girl. The name under the picture was Marika.

"Where did you get that?"

"She left it for me. After she left the rectory that time I found this on the floor. You see, she's the devil. Or the man she was with. He was the devil and she works for him. It makes sense, Frank. It really makes sense if you think about it. There's Dahlgren and he was in league with the devil, and then the devil came himself."

"What did he look like?"

"In the car, I couldn't make him out. When he stood at the rear of the church—he was a young man, average-looking. I don't know."

"Gus, I know how tough your life has been. I know you've been suffering."

"Oh, Frankie—for all these years. My mother wanted me to be a priest, you remember? I never wanted that life. And then Dahlgren—"

"What did Dahlgren do?"

"You know what he did."

"No."

"You were there."

"We did a lot of things, Gus. We were kids."

"I was so naïve. Pure. You know that. Remember?"

"We called you Father Magpie..."

"Yes. You did. All the kids on Mirror Street. And that used to make Jack angry. Remember that?"

"He wasn't angry. He liked to kid you. He loved you, Gus. We all did. Bobby Mack's daughter came to visit you?"

"I tried to help her, sad kid. But what could I do? I can't help myself. Even Greenfield Bob is cursed. We're all cursed. Only the blood of Christ can wash us clean..."

"It makes me very sad, Gus."

"I know. I know. God will take care of it. He'll take care of you and me and Greenfield Bobby Mack and his daughter. God will take care of all of us. Christ will take care of all of us."

"And Dahlgren? And Eggerman?"

"This is God's way," Father Magoczy said. He pushed the beer away from him. "I love you, Frank. I'll always love you. We all loved each other. There was a great love there. But Satan was also there. We're out of touch..."

"You've said that. Out of touch with what?"

"God. God's mercy, God's grace. My poor discarded baby..." He smiled wanly. "Anything else, Frank?"

"I don't think so. For now."

They left the bar. "Do you have your car?"

"I walked," Father Magoczy said.

"I'll drive you back to the rectory."

"I want to walk."

"It's raining."

"Not so hard. It feels good. How long are you going to be in the Burg?"

"I'm not sure. I want to find who killed Dahlgren and the Egg."

"I understand. They're in a better place now."

"Dahlgren, too?"

"I don't know. I used to pray for him. Perhaps I helped. Pray for me, Kalin."

"I will."

"I'll pray for you."

They embraced. Kalinyak watched his old friend move slowly, steadily down the street. He did not turvn back. He continued walking until he was lost in mist and darkness.

Chapter
Twelve

Kalinyak checked into the Mountain Inn, the same motel on the edge of town where he had stayed before. He slept poorly. He dreamed of the shack in Oil City, huge snarling dog charging the fence. He awoke in a sweat. He finally fell back asleep. At a point near dawn, his daughter stood at the foot of the bed, looking sad, infinitely sad, humming something. "You're out of touch," she sang.

He got up, dressed, and drove back toward Oil City. It had stopped raining, but the day was gray and cold. He walked up the asphalt-and-mud path to the shack. In the gray morning light, it looked less ominous. The sleek ebony-and-gray mastiff charged the fence, barking and slathering. "Hey, doggie," Kalinyak said. The dog barked louder, a pained, ripping sound.

A curtain behind the front window parted for an instant. Someone was watching him. "Hey!" he called. "Anybody there?"

The door opened. A woman stood in a heavy, quilted housecoat. Wrinkled, old, she wore thick make-up. "I'm looking for Steve," Kalinyak said.

"He's not here." The woman spoke in a quiet voice, a surprisingly youthful voice.

"Where is he?"

"I don't know. He hasn't been here for a while."

"How long?"

"He comes and goes. It's been a while."

"You're his mother?"

"Yes."

"The German girl? Have you seen her?"

The woman didn't speak for a moment. She mouthed something wordlessly, a mutter. "She's a whore," the woman said.

"Your son's girlfriend...?"

"She's using him, has her hooks in him."

"What can you tell me about her?"

"Nothing. She's a whore."

"How well did you know her?"

"Well enough. Crazy, vicious whore. Everything she's done. What do you want from me?"

"I don't want anything. I just want to find your son. And the girl."

"I tried to do my best," the woman said.

"I'm sure you did."

"I tried to protect him. When he was a kid, they used to taunt him. He didn't have a happy childhood." She gazed at Kalinyak and her eyes were wide and disturbing, almost plaintive, and he felt uneasy and sad. "He means well. You don't know. No one knows..."

"I'm sorry."

She turned from him. He could see she was crying. Kalinyak wanted to approach her and comfort her, but the large dog stood tense, quivering; his yellow eyes never left Kalinyak.

"Can I come back at some other time?"

She shook her head. "I'm...out of time..."

"What do you mean? Are you ill?"

"Yes. Ill. I forgive you..." She backed away into the shack.

"Ma'am?" Kalinyak called out. "Please, ma'am ..."

The mastiff watched him with statuesque indifference. The shack was quiet. He turned and walked down the hill, moved and disturbed. Who was this woman? What did it all mean, all she said about her son and Marika and her life? What should he do?

On the drive back to Pittsburgh, his mind raced. There had been something eerie and pathetic about this woman, deeply troubling. Did she know where the German girl was?

He lay on his bed in the hotel staring at the ceiling. He could not sleep. *I'm out of time, the woman had said. And Magpie had said he was out of touch. And his daughter in his dream had sung, you're out of touch. And some time past, some time past Doyle Eggerman had said of his wife, She's out of touch. And the killer had scrawled on mirrors, baby, your out of time. Mirrors. Mirror Street. What had Bobby Mack said? Mirror Street. You'd think with a name like that, you could hold the street up to your face and see what the hell you were about. Not Mirror Street. Should have called it Smoke and Mirror Street.*

The phone was ringing. Kalinyak jolted awake, alarmed. He hadn't realized he had fallen asleep.

It was Cory in the lobby. "Can I come up?"

"What time is it?"

"Nearly two a.m. I need a place to sleep. Please."

"No. I'll be right down."

Cory was seated in one of the thick lobby chairs, hunched, tense. His eyes were dark and bloodshot like he hadn't had a night's rest in days. Kalinyak noticed there was a tremor in his hands. "What am I going to do?" he said.

"What do you mean?"

Cory smiled. It was thin and not very attractive. "You visited my mother? Why?"

"How did you know?"

"I called her. I always do. I'm all she has. She always meant well. She had a tough life."

"You had a tough life."

"What doesn't break me makes me stronger," he said so quietly it was almost inaudible.

"Where's Marika?"

"I can't find her. I've been looking. Everyone's looking."

"Something's going on here. Tell me. What do you have to do with her?"

He shook his head. "I barely know her. That's the god's honest truth. Everyone thinks I'm close to her, that we have a thing. It's not true. Like everyone, I've never felt comfortable with her."

"You drove her up to see the priest, Father Magoczy."

"I did her a favor. She gave me some bucks for it."

"Twice. What did she want with him?"

"She's very religious—she says. Somehow she knew this man. She wanted something from him—I don't know."

"Did she talk about Dahlgren to you?"

"Yes. She said he beat her up once. She despised him."

"Eggerman? My friend, Doyle?"

"No. I don't recall that she did."

"You're in some trouble, you know?"

"How's that?"

"You have this relationship. Your girlfriend is the chief suspect in two horrendous murders."

"She's not my girlfriend. I told you. I barely know her. I don't even know her last name. I don't even know where she lives. She would just pop up from time to time in my life. I never knew when she'd be there. I never knew how she got there. She was just this very freaky lady. She was a hooker, but she didn't have a hooker's personality. She wasn't a junkie, as far as I could tell. She wasn't doing what she did for the money. I don't know. Just very mysterious."

"Why don't you come down to Ross Street with me. We'll talk to some people."

"At this hour?"

"There'll be someone to talk to."

"If you think it would help—I'm having a tough time of it these days. They've just scared everyone away. I need—I need—"

"To work your hustles, right?"

"I miss my friends," he said with a wan smile.

They walked over to the courthouse, the police section. Several of the homicide detectives working the case were there. They took Cory into an interrogation room. Kalinyak watched through a one-way mirror.

A while later, Bobby Mack joined him in the narrow cubicle behind the mirror. Stupka, the police chief, was with him. "What'd they do? Wake you?"

"Hey," said Bobby, "if this thing breaks, me and the chief'll want to get our pictures taken. Hanratty'll be here soon."

"They're trying to sober him up now," Stupka said with a laugh.

"What do you think, Frankie?" Bobby Mack said.

"I don't think there's anything here. You never know, though," Kalinyak said. "Is it possible this girl did this all herself? Or is there someone working it with her? Damndest thing."

"You definitely never know," Stupka said. He lit up a thin, black stogie, a Marsh Wheeling.

The interrogation droned on. They could hear it through a speaker next to the glass. "I swear to you, I don't really know her," Cory was saying. "I told you alls I know. Hey, crazy bitch going around chilling people, I'm going to tell you, right? Could happen to me. I just don't know that much about her."

"When she come to the country?" the detective in the interrogation room said.

"Have no idea. Think she mentioned something about marrying a soldier from this area. I just don't know."

"Where was she living?"

"I thought someplace in West Virginia."

"Did she have kids?"

"I don't know."

"A phone? Surely she had a phone."

"No."

"How would you contact her?"

"She would find me."

"What did she want with you?"

"I felt in some crazy way she was lonely. She might have been a model or something at one time."

"Why do you say that?"

"She just was—I don't know, watching herself in the mirror all the time. Fashion conscious."

"What would you talk about?"

"Not much."

"She mention Dahlgren?"

"A few times. I think he had beaten her up."

"Eggerman?"

"No."

One of the detectives gazed toward the glass. He had a helpless look on his face. "I'll talk to him," Kalinyak said.

"Squeeze him, Kalin," Bobby Mack said.

"I don't want to scare him off. I don't want him calling for a lawyer."

"No," Stupka said. "We don't want that."

Kalinyak entered the interrogation room. He nodded to the detectives and they left. "They treat you all right?"

"Yes. The truth is I don't know anything."

"They think because you knew the girl—"

"Of course. They think I know something. And I don't. I don't know squat about her."

"She ever talk about offing someone?"

"No."

"Display anger against certain people?"

"No. Well, just Dahlgren. She was upset because he had beaten her up one time. She wouldn't go into it."

"You said you thought she was from West Virginia. What gave you that idea?"

"She must have said some things. I don't remember specifically. She talked about hillbillies. I just got this idea she was from around Wheeling. In that area."

"Why would you think that?"

"Nothing specific. She must have said something."

"Like what would she say?"

"We didn't talk very much."

"You have a thing with her?"

"A thing?"

"Sexual thing."

"Not really."

"What does that mean?"

"She wanted to. We messed around a bit. But nothing really to write home about."

"When you did talk, what would you talk about? You see what I'm doing here—"

"Not really."

"I'm looking for anything, any clue, no matter how small."

"I can only help you with what I know—"

"Which is?"

"Which is I met her, I don't know, a couple of months ago. Didn't particularly like her, she wasn't my type. She somehow latched on to me, not in any big way. We'd see each other maybe once a week, if that. She'd leave and I just assumed she lived in West Virginia or near West Virginia."

"She give you any money?"

"She may have, a few dollars here and there. She didn't like faggots. I think she enjoyed the fact—she just enjoyed, whatever."

"The fact what?"

"I don't know."

"That you enjoyed bashing fags?"

"She may have liked that."

"Can I be honest with you, Cory? Something doesn't sit right here. Something's not right. You know this girl months now and you know nothing about her. How'd she get around?"

Cory shrugged. "Car, I guess."

"What kind of car?"

"I never saw it."

"Isn't that a little strange?"

"Look, I'd come to the Aida or the place on Ninth. Or over on The Strip and nine times out of ten she was already there working some hustle or other. We'd hook up for a little bit—if we went any place it was in my car. For all I know, she took the Greyhound to get to town. You know, I, ah—"

"What?"

"Could use a little something to eat."

"Such as?"

"Couple hamburgers'd be good."

"This hour, they'd have to be White Tower."

"I love White Tower."

"Some fries?"

"Double fries. And one of those thick malts. Strawberry."

Kalinyak came out of the interrogation room. The two homicide detectives went back into the room. Kalinyak huddled with Stupka, Bobby Mack, and Hanratty. "We're not getting anything here. Waste of fucking time," Stupka said.

A delivery boy arrived with the sandwiches. Kalinyak took them into the interrogation room. The detectives left once again. Cory tore into the food.

"You were hungry."

"Starved."

Kalinyak didn't speak for a while as Cory chowed down. "For Chrissake, Cory—give us something. Anything."

"I'd love to. I don't know anything."

"Okay, let's put it this way—do you think Marika, this girl, is capable of killing people?"

"I wouldn't have thought it, no. But it looks like she is. Which is scary because it means we can never judge a book by its covers." He didn't talk for a while. He sipped hard on his malted. "I've been having it tough. I'm telling you the truth. My livelihood has been just cut to nothing."

"Hustling fags?"

"If you want to say that, yes. Yes, that's my livelihood."

"You never did anything else?"

"I wanted to be a graphic artist. I studied in the Art Institute over on Grant Street. I was there for almost two years. I had to quit. It was too tough, working, paying for school. Through a teacher at the Institute, I fell into the scene, the Aida scene, Hot Box scene. And I could make some good bucks. I never gave my career a chance."

"How often do you see your mother?"

He didn't speak for a long moment. "I see her every once in a while. She's had a tough time of it."

"Where's your father?"

Again, he didn't speak for a long while. "I never knew him. My mother had me when she was eighteen. She had a tough time of it."

"You have no father?"

"I'm a bastard. Yes."

"No idea who your father was?"

"No."

"Someone said, someone told me that your mother— worked out of her house there. Was a professional..."

"She did what she had to do. I don't condemn her for it. It was difficult growing up, people there at all hours, ridicule at school. If it doesn't break you, it makes you stronger."

"Okay, Cory. We're finished for now."

He walked Cory to the door. In the hall, Stupka and Bobby Mack stood watching. Hanratty had arrived and he was standing with them. Kalinyak took some money out of his pocket and gave it to Cory. "Get yourself a room and a good meal."

"Thank you."

He hurried away down the hall. "What was that?" Hanratty said.

"I'll make out a chit."

"Jesus Christ," Hanratty said with a wink toward Bobby Mack, "you're a good time Charlie."

The four moved down the hall to Stupka's office. On a table was an assortment of weapons—handguns, rifles, knives, clubs. "The fishing expedition," Stupka said.

Kalinyak studied the guns. Three of them were 9mm and could have been the weapon the German had pulled on him. "Anything on these?" he said, indicating the guns.

"No line on anything yet. We're still trying to track them down."

"Jesus," Bobby Mack said. "Why'd they rouse me so early?"

"He might have starting spilling his guts," Kalinyak said. "He seemed to have been in that kind of mood. But I'll be honest with you—I don't think he's involved. I kind of believe him—"

"What does that mean?" Hanratty said. " 'Kind of believe him?' "

"Well, with these people, anything's possible. How can you tell they're lying? Their lips are moving. But, I think he genuinely barely knows this woman. Just the way he talked about her. Feeling of alienation from her. That's the way most people seem to have reacted to her. She's a psycho."

"No doubt about it," Hanratty said.

"This is strange. This is very unusual," said Stupka. "Usually women, when they kill, it's for a very specific reason. Man cheated on her, abused her. Whatever."

"She obviously has a reason," Hanratty said. "If she did these killings alone, she knew Dahlgren and Doyle."

"There was some link there."

"Okay," said Bobby Mack. "We have this hooker. Dahlgren beats her out of money or something, beats her up. She wants to cut of his balls. Where does Eggerman come into this?"

"Suppose the two of them have this thing with her?" Hanratty said. "Maybe Dahlgren is the one who does her wrong, but the Egg is implicated. Guilt by association. What he does is so terrible, it drives her to murder."

"Grotesque murder like this? Castration?" Bobby Mack said. "Hour glass? Writing in blood on the mirror? This is the work of a homicidal maniac. This is beyond just payback."

Kalinyak pulled on a pair of styrene gloves from a cardboard box on the table and picked up several of the guns. "Yeah, one of these, I bet." He looked over at Bobby Mack. "If you're right, if this some sort of maniac, and it sure seems like it is, the killer isn't finished."

"That's what I've been thinking," Stupka said. "That's why we've been flooding all of the bars and clubs in that area from the Triangle to Polish Hill. Keep a strong presence there."

"Good, good," said Hanratty.

"Yeah," Bobby Mack said, "this freak isn't finished..."

He and Kalinyak walked back to the Forrest Harris Hotel. "I want to unwind," Bobby Mack said. "When they called me before, I wasn't asleep. I couldn't sleep."

"I understand."

"Jack. Then Doyle. Who would have ever thought?" They entered the hotel lobby and stood just beyond the great, brass revolving door. "And I worry about my daughter. She's mired in this world of pimps and whores. Mary, mother of God."

"I need to get sleep," Kalinyak said.

"Well, I'm going to begin my day." Kalinyak started for the elevator bank. Bobby Mack walked with him. "What keeps going round and round in my head," he said, "is the relationship between Jack and the Egg. What could it have been? How could they have been tied together like that in death? There's something there, Kalin."

"It's like a knot. We've got to separate out the strands. You get cases like this. I had a thing on an Indian reservations just outside Tucson. Five, six people involved. Family thing. With my daughter—there was this kid down the end of the block, Seventh Day Adventist kid, very religious...this came out years later... It's all knotted up."

Bobby Mack stopped. "God," he said.

"What?" Kalinyak turned. Bobby's daughter, Lisa, was seated just opposite the elevator bank.

Chapter Thirteen

Bobby Mack stood by the elevators, his face flushed, as Kalinyak moved to Mack's daughter. Her make-up was streaked, her pupils dilated. Her head kept dipping toward her lap in a junkie nod. "Lisa?" Kalinyak said.

Speech slurred, voice low, hoarse, almost inaudible, she fought to keep her eyes open. "Cory was calling me on my cell phone earlier. Kept calling. Wanted to meet me here."

"What for?"

"Money. What else? I shined him on. And then later I started to think about it and I came over." She pulled herself upright, rubbed her nose with her hand. "He—ah— wasn't here. Desk clerk said that you were out. I—ah— thought I'd wait for you."

Bobby Mack had moved closer; he stood several feet away. "Look at you," he said. "Jesus Christ!"

"Don't take the Lord's name in vain." She looked up at Kalinyak. "I didn't know you'd be with this prick."

Bobby Mack looked lost. His breathing was labored. "What do you want from me? What?"

She laughed and he started to say something. He caught himself and moved away. "Nothing I can do," he said to himself.

Kalinyak put his arm on Bobby Mack's shoulder. He stared into his eyes. There was a profound sadness there; it was unsettling and Kalinyak was moved for his friend. "Stay with her for a little while," Kalinyak said.

"What for? So she can call me a prick and an asshole? So she can tell me how I wrecked her life?"

Standing now, Bobby Mack's daughter screamed: "You did wreck my life!"

"Jesus!"

"That's right. You! You did it!"

"Jesus Christ." Bobby Mack turned to Kalinyak. In his eyes there were pain and sadness and confusion. Bobby shook his head and walked quickly from the lobby.

"You shouldn't talk to your father like that," Kalinyak said, moving to the girl. She sank back onto the lobby couch. She didn't look at him. Her head moved up and down in a slow heroin nod. "Lisa?"

"I'm Lara," she said. "Like Doctor Zhivago."

"Why talk to your father like that?"

"What difference does it make?" She hummed softly. "I'm tired. I've been thinking about Cory and his girlfriend. They're in this together. They were setting these guys up. It's all about money."

"How?"

"They were setting them up for something, and it went bad, and so they did what they did."

"Dahlgren first. Then Eggerman. No."

"They're in this together. I'm sure of it. They're in it together."

"He says she wasn't his girlfriend."

"Maybe not. Maybe they're just working together."

"Kill the goose that laid the golden egg? Makes no sense." He stood above her. She was looking in the direction where her father had departed. "Want to get something to eat?"

"No." She rose and walked slowly toward the revolving door. "I got a job waiting for me." At the great brass door, she turned. "They were setting those fuckers up."

She moved off into the night, and Kalinyak took the elevator to his room and stretched out on the bed fully clothed. He looked at the pictures of his dead daughter, looked at them one by one as though she were alive. He wanted to talk to her. He fell asleep.

He awoke after a few hours. He had been dreaming. He couldn't remember what it was, but it left him anxious. He showered and shaved, put on a change of clothes. It was nearly seven o'clock. He called Bobby Mack at the Courthouse building. "Helleva night's sleep," Bobby said.

"I feel like I should be doing something."

"I'll pick you up. We have someone to visit."

In Bobby Mack's car, not the town car, but his official car, he explained: "Last night someone came up with a possibility to explore. Gun dealer who thinks he might have seen the German. He sold one of the 9mms."

The morning was cold and gray. Kalinyak was sorry he hadn't brought his jacket. "Looks like snow," he said.

"Weather report said there might be something, first of the season," Bobby Mack said.

The gun shop was on the North Side, across the Seventh Street Bridge. It was still too early, so they stopped for breakfast at a diner on Sandusky Street not far from the river.

When they finished, it was a little after nine. "Let's check out this pup," Bobby Mack said, draining his coffee cup.

They drove up River Avenue along the Allegheny through an area that once was heavy industry, but was now largely desolate. The great mills were dark and rusting. It had started to snow. In a side street, they found the gun shop.

The owner was a small, bald man with thick glasses. "I already talked to the detectives," he said, after Bobby Mack had displayed his identification.

"We're interested in the girl," Bobby Mack said.

"Kind of nice-looking. Hard," he said. "Spoke with an accent. Wanted a German gun."

"When was this?"

"Three months ago. I can get the exact date. I gave it to the detective."

"That's all right. The gun was—"

"Heckler & Koch 9mm. The P-9. This was a rebuilt model. Was a nice model, stainless steel. Well, you saw it. Was expensive."

"How did she pay you?"

"She tried to bargain. She led me to believe that she would, ah, trade certain favors, if I cut the price—"

"Did you?" Bobby Mack said.

"No, no. You know there're all these diseases. She was nice-looking, though. No, I'm a happily married man. Certainly no."

"Did she give an address, phone number?" Kalinyak said.

"She did," Bobby Mack said. "Address turned out to be Pine Valley. Phone number, the Hot Box."

"Anything else you can tell us?"

"No. I just remember her because she was good-looking and she offered, you know, something in payment, you know. Also, she had this look—"

"Look?"

"Something funny in the eyes. Cold, blue. Penetrating. Scary."

They left. It was snowing harder now. "Let's ride out to Pine Valley," Kalinyak said.

Pine Valley was quiet. There were a few young ladies there, several men in business suits. An old-time rock-and-roll was coming from the juke box, The Rolling Stones. Two of the girls were dancing with each other, doing a sixties boogaloo.

They sat in a booth. Bobby Mack ordered a scotch. Kalinyak had a coke. "What do you think?" Bobby Mack said.

"I don't know what to think."

"Look at this place. Hasn't changed at all. It's like a time capsule. Even the jukebox. Like we're in a time warp."

"She came here, knew this place months ago. Gave the address to the gun store man. Buys a gun. Starts hanging out at hooker joints, fag joints. Hooks up with Cory, more or less. He says they never really had much of a relationship."

"But they spent time together."

"He said he thought she was lonely. He was lonely, no doubt about that. Two lonely people in this world. Your daughter's in that scene, too. She knew both of these people."

"What the hell happened? What the hell happened?" Bobby Mack said. "She hooks up with this guy, kind of hooks up with him, meets Jack Dahlgren, he beats her up. She kills him. All right. She's pissed off. She not only kills him, she tortures him. Okay. Now how in the name of hell did Eggerman get involved? How?"

They got up and walked outside. The snow was falling in thick waves. They strolled around the Pine Valley building. They gazed over at the row of motels that lined the road leading to Pine Valley. At the rear of the place, Kalinyak came to a sudden halt. "What?" Bobby Mack said.

"Magpie's car." His green Dodge was parked in a far space at the edge of the lot.

Kalinyak and Bobby Mack hurried back into the club. The bartender remembered the priest. "He came in three hours ago. Had a drink, Imp 'n Iron. Looked like he was waiting for someone. Woman comes in. He sees her and moves to her."

"Woman? The blonde woman from a few weeks ago?"

"Dunno. I didn't really notice."

"We talked to you after the murder down the road—" Kalinyak said.

"That's right. I remember."

"This priest was in here that day."

"That's right. Yes."

"He was supposed to meet a woman, but they missed each other. Was this the same woman?"

"I didn't notice. Really. I was setting up the girls' drinks over there. You know, they were having, well, you know those women's kind of drinks. They had two White Cadillacs, A Golden Dream, one had a, what was it? Some liqueur drink or other, an Orange Blossom...I saw the Father get up and he was walking toward the door and this lady was moving out the door with him."

"What color hair?" Kalinyak said.

"Couldn't tell. Had on a big hat. Fur coat."

"Good, thank you," Kalinyak said and he and Bobby Mack hurried from the club. They jogged to the motel next door. The desk clerk, a lean, consumptive-looking man with pencil-thin moustache, plastered-down black hair, striped shirt, red bowtie, sat painfully erect behind the counter. He was watching a soap opera on a small set above the sign-in desk.

Bobby Mack flashed his ID, leaned across the desk, and in a low voice questioned the clerk. Bobby Mack's face was flushed a deep red. His breathing was labored. Had a priest or a blonde woman checked in recently? No priest, no blonde. No woman in a fur coat and white hat. "Look at this," the man said, indicating the television set. "This is a pisser. See that woman? The nurse? She's a deadbeat. She'll get hers..."

They rushed from the motel. A terrible feeling of impending doom came over Kalinyak. Though he wasn't a believer, he found himself praying for Magoczy.

They looked down Route 19. The road was filled with snow. The trees overhanging the road were heavy with snow. The snow continued to fall, providing a scrim of white in front of Motel Row--the Alpine Cottages, Valley Arms, Scottish Inn, a half dozen more places up and down the roadway.

They went from motel to motel. The fifth motel they tried, the clerk said, "Girl came in early this morning, rented a room. Couple of hours later, I saw her drive off."

"What kind of car?"

"Couldn't tell you. Just saw her get in a car and drive off. It just registered, that's all. She was nice-looking."

"What room was she in?"

"53. Second floor all the way at the end."

He called his staff supervisor and a maid was sent to meet them at the room. She unlocked the door, started in, gasped and turned away. Kalinyak pushed into the room.

Kalinyak and Bobby Mack stood in the doorway staring at the grotesque scene. They did not move or talk.

Father Augustus Magoczy was spread eagle, nude, on the bed. His eyes were wide with horror. The mirror was smeared with blood, words written in blood. The bed was red with blood.

"Oh, my God. Oh, dear God," Bobby Mack moaned. "Dear, Jesus. Oh, God."

The wind blew. The snow fell furiously. Bobby Mack hurried to the bathroom. Kalinyak could hear him throwing up.

Chapter Fourteen

Funeral services for Father Augustus Magoczy took place in the Hungarian Church of St. Marek Krizin on Saline Street in Greenfield, just off Four Mile Run Road. A number of old-time Greenfield Hungarians who had been friendly with Magpie's family showed up for his funeral, as did many of the Mirror Street Aces.

The Aces appeared stunned, mortified. This was the third member of the old gang to be brutally murdered. What was going on? Kalinyak and Bobby Mack, as the remaining two Huns, were devastated. "What does it mean?" Bobby Mack said. "Is it a business thing? All right. Jack Dahlgren. That's understandable. But Doyle? Magpie?"

"What about the church?" Kalin said. "What happened with St. Philomena's?"

"Someone's murdering for that?"

"I don't know what you all did. I don't know the intricacies."

"Business! Simple, honest business deal..."

Magpie's family had long since scattered and disintegrated. The only living member in Pittsburgh was his mother, who was now near ninety and senile. None of his brothers or sisters came to the funeral.

Before the priest could begin the service, Rosa Magoczy wandered to the front of the church and began chanting in a high, barely comprehensible, accented voice: "St. Philomena, pray for us. St. Philomena, filled with the most abundant graces from your very birth, pray for us. St. Philomena, faithful imitator of Mary, pray for us!"

A young priest rushed to her and tried to lead her back to her seat. She went on, louder now, ancient lady, ramrod erect, babushka on her head, woolen coat over a polka dot cotton dress, screaming now: "St. Philomena, model of Virgins, pray for us. St. Philomena, victim of the love of Jesus, pray for us. St. Philomena, invincible champion of chastity, pray for us..."

Another priest came to her. He held her and tried to sooth her. She continued in a high wail: "St. Philomena, scourged like your Divine Spouse, pray for us. St. Philomena, pierced by a shower of arrows, pray for us. St. Philomena, consoled by the Mother of God, when in chains, pray for us..."

Several nuns had joined the battle. One of the nuns forced a pill into her mouth. They managed to get her seated.

She went on quieter now, a mumble: "St. Philomena, cured miraculously in prison, pray for us. St. Philomena, comforted by angels in your torments, pray for us. St. Philomena, whose name is glorified in Heaven and feared in Hell, pray for us. St. Philomena, who preferred torments and death to the splendors of a throne, pray for us. St. Philomena, all powerful with God, pray for us..."

The service was rapid and perfunctory, done mainly in Latin and Hungarian. Father Gilchristie, who had officiated eloquently at Doyle Eggerman's funeral, was ill, and a replacement, Father Biku Karas, had come down from Altoona to help nudge Magpie toward heaven. Nearly as old as Magpie's mother, Father Karas was circumspect about the dead priest's boozing: "He had his devils, and he fought the good fight with them constantly—" His most precious quality was his humility. Here several of the Aces nodded in agreement. The high point of his life was the time spent at Clarion State Teachers College when, in his senior year, he made second-string linebacker on the football team.

The service over, the cortege drove along Hazelwood Avenue, up the hill to Calvary Cemetery. The day was gray. Heavy cloud loomed low in the sky. It had been snowing ever since Magoczy's murder, cold, granular scatterings which barely covered the roadway.

At the cemetery atop Calvary Hill, it was windy, and the grains of snow stung the faces of the mourners.

Less than a dozen people had come to the cemetery: Kalinyak and Bobby Mack, Betty Malloy, Kari Eggerman, Tito Bronk and his wife, Buddha Kruisper, several others. Kalinyak looked into the faces of his old friends, and there was a blasted expression there, something stunned and confused and frightened. What did this mean?

After, Kalinyak and Bobby Mack and Betty Malloy had dinner at Politos on Forbes Street. No one spoke for a very long time. Lucy, the owner, came to the table and began to joke with Bobby Mack, and then she realized that something serious was going on.. "Gus Magoczy was murdered," Betty Malloy said.

"Oh, my God!"

"Did you know him?"

"Of course I knew him. Gussie. He was good friends with my son, Ron. They all played football together. And then Ron even went to Clarion with Gussie. Magpie! What happened?"

"It's this thing that's occurring," Bobby Mack said. "Someone killed, you know—"

"Yes, yes, of course. Eggerman. The Egg. And your ex—" This said to Betty Malloy: "Jackie Dahlgren. Who's doing this? What is this?"

Betty Malloy shrugged, looked uncomfortable.

"I liked this Magpie. He was a sweet kid. He became a priest. I remember. He liked to have a drink now and then. He would come in here occasionally. Not too often in recent years. That was a sad family, the Magoczys. Father ran off, they all went in different directions. The mother, she's in a home, I heard. When they sold St. Philomena's, she took that very hard. Pushed her over the edge. So they killed the Magpie!" She shook her head and made a soft tutting sound.

The table lapsed into silence. A waiter appeared. "Karl, take good care of these people," Lucy Polito said.

"We'll have some drinks. Then we'll see about food. Imp 'n Iron for me," Bobby Mack said. "Double Imp. Betty?"

"The same."

"Frank?" Lucy said.

"Yeah. I'll have the same..."

"Now that's the Frankie Kalin we all knew and loved," Bobby Mack said. He lit up a Camel, blew smoke in the air, offered one to Kalinyak, who took it and rapidly lit up and seemed to devour the cigarette.

The drinks arrived. Lucy Polito brought over a large dish of fried calamari. "Something to nibble till you figure out what you're going to eat."

Kalinyak took the double Imperial whiskey in one long swallow. He sipped at the Iron City beer. Betty and Bobby Mack also downed their drinks quickly. Lucy brought them a bottle of Imperial and several more Iron Cities. "If you're going to be serious about this, let's be serious," she said. "Who's driving?"

"I am," Bobby Mack said.

"That's good. You can hold your booze. You always could. I wish you had been here that night when Ronnie, you know—"

"I wish I had been here, too."

"So many years ago! And now Jack Dahlgren and Doyle and Gussie are gone..." She sighed and stood there for a moment. "You want to order food now?"

"I think later," Betty Malloy said. Lucy moved off.

"There were five Huns," Bobby Mack said quietly. "Now there are two. What's going on?"

"You think it has something to do with the Huns?" Kalinyak said. "What? What about the Huns? What's happening?"

"And you," Betty Malloy said. "You haven't been here in years and years. Jack and Doyle—they had business together. Father Gus had nothing to do with them."

"The German girl visited him twice," Kalinyak said.

"You think the three were involved with this girl?" Betty Malloy said.

Kalinyak felt as though his head would fly apart. He could feel the blood pounding behind his eyes. "They all met her. She called them and they met her. And they met her at Pine Valley. Why? What does Pine Valley and Jack and Doyle and Father Gus—what is it there?"

He hadn't had liquor in almost six years. He knew it wasn't good for him. He poured himself another drink.

They ordered several pasta dishes and barely touched them. They finished off the bottle of Imperial Whiskey. They started out of the restaurant.

"I have this terrible feeling," Kalinyak said. "I'm not used to drinking. I feel like my world is flying apart."

"I feel this, too," Bobby Mack said. "I can't grab hold of any of this. Jack, Doyle, Father Gus. What does it mean? What does it mean?"

When they got to Betty Malloy's house, she looked over at Frank and held his arm. "Do you want to come in?"

Bobby Mack said, "It's a good thing, Kalin. I have Theresa waiting for me. You need someone to talk to. This is a cataclysm here."

Kalinyak and Betty got out of the town car and started up the walk to her house. There was a thick layer of snow on the walk. It was still coming down slowly, feathery flakes now.

Kalinyak turned to Bobby Mack, who sat in the car staring straight ahead. "Are you all right, Bob?"

Bobby Mack turned to him. "I don't know what this means, Frankie. Who's next? You or me?"

"We have to be careful," Frank said.

"Yes." Bobby Mack drove off. Betty was waiting at the door. Kalinyak staggered up the walk to her. He slipped on the snow, but caught himself. "I'm drunk," he said.

She opened the door and he followed her into the house. She led him into the bedroom. They embraced. "We've had so much death," she said. "When someone dies you want to know you're alive."

They kissed and he eased her back onto the bed. He undressed her. Her body was astonishing, sleek, youthful. She gazed at him, a sly smile on her face.

They made love. It was filled with sadness and pain.

Chapter Fifteen

|||

He awoke to the smell of bacon, which was not pleasant. There was a heaviness in the air in the room. His head throbbed. He felt jangly, nerves raw, an electric uneasiness that spread through his whole body.

He swung his legs off the edge of the bed: everything swayed; the floor seemed to fall away. He thought he might throw up.

Magoczy's death weighed on him terribly, more than Dahlgren's, more even than Doyle's. What did it mean?

He showered and came downstairs. Betty was putting breakfast on the kitchen table. "I'll just have some coffee," Kalinyak said.

"We did all right last night," she said.

"Did we?"

"As much as I can remember."

"Whew, my head. Not like in days gone by."

"Tell me about it."

She brought aspirin and a glass of water to him. He gathered her into his arms and kissed her. It felt warm, comfortable. "Betty Malloy," he said.

"Frankie Kalin."

"Who would have thought it?"

She laughed. "When I was a kid I used to think that some day we'd get together. You never paid much attention to me."

"You were so young..."

"Didn't stop Jack."

"Nothing stopped Jack. This life," he said.

"This life."

They both laughed. He sipped on his coffee.

She shook her head. "Scary," she said, suddenly serious. "This thing with—I mean, now Magpie. Poor Magpie."

Kalinyak struggled to put things together, to piece this nightmare together, to make sense of it. "Do you ever feel as if the world isn't quite real? Do you ever look around you and wonder if it isn't all a dream?"

"Sometimes. Yes."

"Something here. Something terrible. Something. What?" he said. "What? What is it—this—Three killed like this. Bizarre. Killed in such a brutal, crazed way. Can't just be a coincidence. What is it?"

"You'll catch whoever did this, won't you?" she said. She sounded suddenly very young, as though they were both in school. As though she were in junior high school. "I mean you and Bobby? I mean, the police. Stupka? All of you?"

"Oh, we'll catch whoever did it," he said, and he didn't believe it. What was he doing here? Not with Betty, necessarily—not only with Betty—but here, in Pittsburgh, his old friends brutally murdered, butchered, mocked. And he's trailing the killer. Or is he? Perhaps the killer is trailing him. How had it come to this?

He felt as if a trap in his life had been sprung, as though he were snared in a web of steel. How? How? He could barely breath. Some great terror was choking off his life. He should have never come home.

The phone rang. It was Bobby Mack. "They're having a memorial service for Magpie up in Tracyville this afternoon. Why don't you run up there and see that Gus's things get packed up. See if you can find out something, anything. Want a detective to go with you?"

"What's the policy?"

"The two guys who caught the case would be willing to go with you. I don't think it's necessary. I think it's better if you scope this out."

After hanging up, Kalin sat with Betty for a while. Suddenly, he felt awkward. "What is it?" she said.

"It's just this place where my life has come. It seems unreal."

"Yes," she said. "Look, there's no obligation here. We had some drinks. We're not kids."

"I know."

"I've always had strong feelings for you."

"I've had them for you."

"So?"

"Okay," he said. And they kissed, but there was a wall between them suddenly and they both felt it and they grew quiet.

"Don't worry about it," Betty said at last.

"All right."

* * *

Nearly a half-foot of snow had fallen overnight. Betty's street looked magical. The great spruce trees were heavy with snow.

She drove him to his hotel. Steam rose from the downtown streets. "I'll talk to you later," he said.

She smiled. "Frank, don't worry about this. Okay?"

"Okay."

He drove up to Tracyville. It had stopped snowing, and the highway had been cleared, but the countryside was brilliant with white. At the church, there was a handful of people for Father Magoczy's memorial. Father Karas spoke again, and since the crowd was limited, his remarks, too, were limited. He did talk of Magpie's humility and his glory as a second string linebacker for Clarion State.

Lud Chamerek, the owner of Café Rusniaki, sat next to Kalinyak. "I didn't know that," he whispered. "He played for Clarion?"

"Yes."

"Funny. Would have never thought old Father Magoczy was an athlete."

"He was a good athlete. Football. Baseball, too. Good field, no hit."

"Ah. This is a tragedy, you know. He was such a harmless man. Who would do this?"

Chamerek invited Kalinyak back to his bar for a bite, but Kalinyak begged off. He had business to take care of.

He spoke with Magpie's housekeeper, and she took him to the rectory, to Gus's room.

The room was a mess, the small bed unmade, books and papers everywhere. "I tried to neaten up for him," the housekeeper said. "He didn't like me coming in here."

She stood there waiting, taking in the room. "I'll have to do some work here," Kalinyak said.

"Fine." She left, and Kalinyak gazed around, not knowing where to start. There was a desk in one corner of the room, and he walked to it and began to go through the stack of papers atop the desk. They were mainly of a religious nature, writings on the church, early saints, the life of Jesus. Magpie had made notes on the papers in a scrawling hand which Kalinyak had difficulty reading.

He found a battered suitcase in the closet and began to fill it with the papers. In a drawer in the desk he found a copy of their high school year book and a stack of composition notebooks.

He leafed through the year book. He found his own picture and an autograph he had scrawled there: "For Magpie. A good friend. Hun till the end! Your friend, Kalin."

He turned to the composition books. There were perhaps a dozen of them. They went back many, many years, to the time when Magoczy entered the seminary. They were rambling attempts at Magpie trying to find his way in this life.

Kalinyak scanned them quickly. Much of what he had written was incomprehensible, written obviously when he had been drinking: "Dahlgren is the devil. I know this now. He has led me here. Deliver me from Evil..." The whole page was filled with the phrase, "Deliver me from Evil." It carried over to the next page and the next, becoming less and less recognizable, until it disintegrated into a scrawl.

In a section of one notebook there were mentions of Pine Valley. Dahlgren and Pine Valley. "You did this to me," was scrawled there. "You are the Devil." And further on down the page: "Out of time. You're out of touch my baby, my poor old fashioned baby, I said baby, baby, baby, you're out of time. Can't make it stop. Stop it. Stop it."

The page was covered with scrawls, "Stop it. Stop it. Stop it."

He turned a page. Written in a shaky hand in blue ink was part of the prayer to St. Philomena that his mother had cried out at his funeral: "St. Philomena, model of Virgins, pray for us. St. Philomena, victim of the love of Jesus, pray for us. St. Philomena, invincible champion of chastity, pray for us..."

He made the long drive back to Pittsburgh in a fog of thought. What did Magpie's writings in the notebooks mean? *Baby, you're out of time!* The exact phrase scrawled in blood on the mirror of the murdered men, including Magpie's murder? What did it mean?

When he arrived in town, he called Bobby Mack. "This is unsettling," he said.

"What?"

"Something bizarre—has to do with Gus. Let's meet."

"Johnny McGuire's?"

"Good."

"What is it?"

"Something crazy. I don't know what to make of it.."

Bobby Mack was already at McGuire's when Kalinyak arrived, seated at a booth in a far corner.

Aside from Bobby, the place was empty of customers. In the dim yellow light reflected off the oak-paneled walls, Bobby Mack looked frozen in gloom. His face was in half shadow. He did not move.

He had a bottle of Imperial whiskey on the table and several bottles of Iron City beer. As Kalinyak arrived at the table, he looked up, and the light glistened off his spectacles. His light blue eyes were watery and dull.

He poured Kalinyak a water glass full of Imperial, offered him a Camel. Kalinyak lit up. He took the smoke deep inside his lungs and felt a certain disgust at himself as well as a deep despair. "What did you find?" Bobby Mack said. His voice was hoarse, tired.

"It's crazy, I don't know. I found these notebooks. They were full of ramblings, you know scrawls, crazy stuff about the devil and such. But also the phrase on the mirrors, *Baby, you're out of time*, "you're" spelled correctly."

"What is that?" Bobby Mack said, stunned. "What the fuck is that?"

"And Pine Valley. There were notes about Pine Valley."

"My God. Frankie, what's going on? Was he in on this thing, in with the German girl? Carrying on something with her? And then she kills him? Is that what it is?"

"He knew about Pine Valley. He knew about the scrawl. I don't know. It's crazy."

Bobby Mack was breathing deeply now. His face was flushed. He had obviously been drinking all day. He lit up another cigarette, stubbed out the one he had been smoking. "Okay, this is what we have—girl kills Dahlgren—"

"Girl lures Dahlgren. We don't know if she killed him. She may have had an accomplice—"

"Magpie? That's ridiculous!"

"How did he know what was scrawled on the mirrors?"

"How old were these notebooks?"

"Some entries were dated. They went back years—"

Bobby Mack rubbed his brow. "Something, something..." he mumbled.

"Okay, let's go back. Let's think back. We have Jack. Doyle. Gussie. Were they in something back, back—?"

"What are you talking about? How far back do you want to go? Where?" Bobby Mack was angry, pained. "Where do you want to go to, Frank?"

"I don't know."

"I don't understand what you're saying—?"

"Look, I've been gone from here years and years now. There may have been something. I don't know. Do you?"

"Dahlgren and the Egg had involvements. I know that. Dahlgren had this weird sexual stuff. Okay. Maybe Doyle was involved in some way. I don't know. But where does Gussie come in? I mean, think Frankie. Think! What're you talking about?"

Kalinyak did not speak. He poured himself another glass of whiskey, downed it quickly. Picked up a cigarette, lit it, then stubbed it out. "Who's next?" Kalinyak said.

"That's what I'm thinking." After a while he said quietly, "I thought I was a tough guy. Greenfield Bobby Mack. No, my father was a tough guy. Nothing would ever get to him. I don't care what it was. My mother died? I don't think he shed a tear. My sister, Cicelia, remember, eighteen years old, killed in that accident, that car crash by the Squirrel Hill bridge. Didn't phase him. That was a tough guy. Me? I worry about Lisa. I worry about my daughter. I worry about all this that's going on. Frankie, I don't understand this. I'm scared. The old Greenfield Bobby Mack, the Old Man, nothing scared him. I'm scared."

"I understand."

"You?"

"Not scared, Bob. Perplexed. Depressed. I'm depressed about what's happened to our friends. And deeply, deeply perplexed."

"Yeah, that, too. But you're not scared?"

"No."

"Okay. You're a better man than I am. I can't sleep no more, unless I kill half a bottle. That's not good."

"No, it's not."

"What can I do? We have to find out what's going on..."

"Yes." Kalinyak stood. "I'm going to go back to the hotel. I still have a ton of Magpie's stuff to look through. And I'm tired."

"I told Phil Hanratty I'd have dinner with him. I think Stupka might be with him. What should I tell them? I don't want to get into this whole Magpie thing. They'll think I'm nuts. We have to figure this out, you and me, Frank. *We* have to figure this out."

"Bobby, we'll figure it."

"Yeah." He looked up at Kalinyak, and his broad, flushed face suddenly looked young and innocent, a kid again. "I miss the Old Man," he said. "The Old Man would know how to figure this. You couldn't slip anything past him. I'm a shadow of him, Kalin. That's the truth."

"You've done all right."

"Naw, I've fucked it all up. Look at my daughter. Look what I did with her."

"Are you going to be all right? You're not going to be driving, are you?"

"Naw. They're meeting me here. Till then, I'll—" He lifted the bottle of Imperial Whiskey and waved it around. "—keep the fucking werewolves at bay..." He laughed, more of a snort than a laugh. His face was flushed a deep red.

Kalinyak got up. "I'm going to get back to Magpie's stuff. It's depressing, you know?"

"I know. Of course. They were sweet guys, Frankie. The Egg. Magpie. Good people. Dahlgren's the only one deserved what he got," He cracked another bottle of beer. "Imp 'n Iron—was there ever anything better in the world?"

Kalinyak returned to his hotel, went to his room. He thought about calling Betty, but he couldn't bring himself to do it. *Baby, you're out of time.* The phrase spun in his mind. What did it mean? How did Magpie come to it so many years before? What did it mean now? What did it mean to the killer?

He looked at the suitcase filled with Magpie's effects, and he wanted to go through them, but he couldn't. Something was holding him back. Was he afraid of what he would find?

He tried to nap. His daughter's face, staring at him from all of her photographs, wouldn't let him sleep.

He walked over to the Aida. The place was busy. Everyone was adjusting to the pressure from the police. He sat at the bar and ordered an Iron City.

He studied the people in the place and disgust came over him. Most of the men and the few women there seemed caricatures of people. Flamboyant, highly made up, exaggerated; they seemed stand-ins for men and women, pretend men and women. And wasn't this true of most? Didn't everyone carry around a mask with them?

Some masks fitted better than others. Phil Hanratty's mask of deputy district attorney was almost a perfect fit. The seriousness, the toughness—was he that way at home? In his pajamas was he that way, making love to his wife, having dinner with his kids? Was he and his mask one and the same thing?

And was Kalinyak's problem the fact that he had a very imperfect mask? What was his mask? Lost loner? Is that the mask he wore or was that the essential *him*. And what did Betty Malloy think of when she saw him? Did she see him or his mask?

Cory was standing next to him. Lost in thought, Kalinyak hadn't seen him approach. He looked wary, tense. "They chilled another one," Cory said. "I guess the cops are getting bored. They've let us alone this past week or so."

"They?"

"She chilled another one. She and someone else. Who knows?"

"Want a drink?" Kalinyak said.

"No. Not right now. I can't stay. Have you seen Lara?"

"Lisa?"

"Lisa, Lara. I need to see her."

"What, you want to beat her up again?"

Cory laughed. It was a harsh laugh. His dark eyes clocked the room, took in everything. "I want to make up to her. I was strung out that night. Well, you saw me. She's a *whoor*, you know. Started giving me shit. But, I was wrong.

She's basically a good kid. I feel bad about it. You know her father, huh?"

"How'd you know that?"

"Little birdie told me. You know how these things get around."

"Marika?"

"Come on. That crazy bitch is long gone. Who knows where she is?"

"Well, she just killed a priest a few days ago."

"You don't know that."

"Okay, she was involved. I think that's safe to say."

"Well, you know what kind of scene we have here—"

"What kind of scene is that?"

"Sick scene. Doesn't take a PhD in psychology to scope that out. No, Lara and I have been in touch. I apologized for what went down. She talked about her father. She had seen him with you a few nights back. It bothered her. You know, kids and their parents—it's a touch and go thing."

"You and your mother?"

"She's had to put up with a lot with me. I don't feel good about it. She raised me, single mom, sacrificed for me. I could have turned out a lot worse. You always feel—" He reached into his pocket and took a cigarette out of a pack. Kalinyak reached for one.

"Since when?"

"Fell off the wagon."

"Impossible to quit, isn't it? They say heroin is easier."

"I doubt that."

"No, they've done studies. Well. I've already resigned myself to lung cancer."

"You were talking about your mother."

"Owe her a lot. Try to make things up to her. In my way, I try. It's very, very difficult."

"What're you doing for money these days?"

He smiled. It was not a pleasant smile. It was tense, twisted. "I get a little help from my friends."

Kalinyak leaned forward as though to embrace him. "Hey," Cory said. Kalinyak patted his jacket at the breast, went under his arms, then down to his waist. He felt the butt of a revolver.

He pulled it out of Cory's waistband, a Harrington & Richardson nickel-plated .38.

"Been knocking over 7-11's?"

"Hey, suppose the bitch decides to do *me*? Figures I'm better off at room temperature? We got us a mad woman out there who knows my name and where to find me. Okay? I gotta run. Gotta find Lara."

"What's your hurry?"

"She owes me some money."

"Owes you?"

"That's right. You find that so hard to believe? In this tight market, I've steered a few things her way. You want to play, you gotta pay."

"Look at me. Look right into my eyes." Cory opened his eyes wide and stared at Kalinyak. His pupils were dark pools; what was reflected there? "Tell me you don't know where the German girl is."

He smiled, but his eyes remained dead. "I don't know where the bitch is. If I knew where she was, the whole world would know. My business can only suffer as long as she's on the loose. You can see this, can't you?"

"Okay."

"I like you," Cory said. "I think you're good people."

"I don't know what to make of you."

"I'm complex."

"I guess so. Well. Enjoy yourself."

"I'm sure I will."

He took the Harrington and Richardson back from Kalinyak; replaced it in his waistband. He exited the place. The bartender came to Kalinyak. "That's a sneaky guy," the bartender said. "Be careful."

"I will." He paid his tab and walked back to the hotel.

In his room once more, he put the suitcase with Magpie's life's detritus on the bed. He opened it and reached in and took a handful of items out.

There were matchbooks and a photograph in a plastic folder. The matchbooks were green with a white pine tree.

The plastic photo folder was white with a green pine tree. All said "Pine Valley" on them.

He opened the photo folder. Six people sat a table. There were drinks on the table, a bottle of Imperial Whiskey, Iron City beer in bottles. The people were high school kids, five boys and a girl. The Huns and Sarah Jo Kazmarek. They were seated next to a juke box.

He lifted a Polaroid picture from the pile. It was Marika, the German girl. Her hair was in a bouffant. She wore a plaid skirt and white blouse. She wore saddle shoes.

He looked at the German girl and then at Sarah Jo. They were the same person.

He opened the yearbook, turned to his entry. Next to his entry was Sarah Jo's entry: "Sarah's the queen of our grade. A better person God never made!" Her blonde hair was in a bouffant. It was the same style as in the Polaroid. Someone, Magpie, Kalinyak assumed, had made a thick black border around the picture with marking pen. Sarah Jo had signed the picture to Gus. "I forgive you," it said. "Sarah Jo."

Kalinyak turned over the Polaroid. On the back was written, "I forgive you. Meet me at Pine Valley ten o'clock in the morning. We have to talk about this."

Underneath the high school picture, Magpie had written: "Out of time. You're out of touch my baby, my poor old fashioned baby, I said baby, baby, baby, you're out of time."

And just below this: "St. Philomena, model of Virgins, pray for us. St. Philomena, victim of the love of Jesus, pray for us. St. Philomena, invincible champion of chastity, pray for us..."

Chapter Sixteen

Kalinyak walked back to Johnny McGuire's. The evening had turned cold. It had started to snow again. His face was numb from the cold. Inside he was numb from what he had found in Magoczy's house. He knew what it was. He knew what it meant. He had to talk to Bobby Mack. He could hear a song playing in his head...

Phil Hanratty and Gene Stupka, the Chief of Police, were seated at the table with Bobby Mack. The Chief was in full uniform. Crab and lobster shells, beer bottles, cigarette butts, littered the table top. There was a second bottle of Imperial Whiskey. Seated next to Bobby was his daughter, Lara.

"Hey, Frank," Hanratty said.

"Kalin," Stupka said.

"How's he doing?" Kalinyak said, nodding toward Bobby. Bobby lifted his head. His eyes were glazed.

"I'll take care of him," Lara said.

"What do you want, Frankie?" Bobby Mack said. His speech was slurred.

"I found some other things. We'll talk tomorrow."

"What other things?"

"We'll talk about it later."

"Wants to dig up the past." He pointed to his head. "I know. I know everything. I knew it all. You didn't remember?"

"Not now, Bobby."

"What's he talking about?"

"Who knows?" Kalin said. "He's drunk."

"Yeah, he's drunk," Bobby Mack said about himself. "Someone wants to kill us, Frank! You and me, we're the only two left. The Huns!" He struggled to get something out of his coat pocket. It was a .38 revolver.

"Hey, Bobby," Hanratty said.

"What do you want?"

"Put that away..."

Bobby Mack waved the gun in the air. "Someone's trying to kill us..."

Lara took his arm and pulled it to her; she placed her hand over the gun. "Put it away, Bob."

"Look who's here, Frankie. My little girl. Honor roll student. Last class they had at St. Philomena's. She was going to do great things."

"C'mon, Bob," Lara said. "We have to go."

Bobby Mack let go of the gun. It fell to the table. Kalinyak reached forward and put it in his pocket.

"We have to go," Bobby Mack said.

"Where?" Kalinyak said.

Bobby Mack put his finger to his lips. Winked. "It's all going to work out, Frank. I got Lisa here. You got it all wrong—this is a good kid. We had a misunderstanding. I love her like my own heart."

Lara looked embarrassed. She shrugged toward Kalinyak. Bobby Mack was on his feet now. Lara helped him to the door. He turned, swayed, and saluted the table. Then he and his daughter went out into the frozen night.

"What was that all about?" Hanratty said.

"Who knows?" Kalinyak said. "We were talking about some things earlier..."

Stupka rose. He also was none too steady. "Have to get home. Got the woman waiting. She has that rolling pin like in the old comics!" He laughed. "What do you think on this thing here? Everyone is up in arms over this. Mayor's going ballistic. 'What is this? Where do you think we are? We don't have things like this, serial murders. This is a Hunky town. Hunkies don't behave this way...' You know this area has never had a serial murderer before? That's for California. Chicago. Up there in Washington State. We have our domestic murders and our robbery murders. Every once in a while a numbers runner would get chilled—that was in the old days. But not no one getting their balls cut off, bloody messages. German *whoor*, madwoman—what is she, left over from the Second World War? Okay, okay—I'm going..."

He pulled himself up straight and walked slowly to the door. He tried to push the door forward, then realized you had to pull it to you. He finally stumbled out into the snowy night.

"Mrs.'s going to kick the shit out of him. You know her—Eloise Moriarty. She was from over there on Four Mile Run."

"I knew her brothers. They ran with Jimmy Flynn."

"That's the ones."

"The big kid, Gene, played football with me. Boxed, too."

"Wanted to become another Billy Conn."

"Yeah, had his ass flattened, first round, South Side Marketplace."

Hanratty was smiling. "Who did that to him?"

"You know who. The Hunky Hurricane, that's who."

"Want a nightcap?"

"Sure."

Hanratty poured a water glass full of Imperial Whiskey. "I hope they don't go there," Hanratty said. "Hope they don't mess things up."

"Go where?"

"Oh, the daughter wants him to go over there, you know where all the action has been? Pine Valley."

"What the hell for?"

"Bobby Mack's kid come here and says she knows someone wants to tell Bobby some things about this whole thing. I says, 'Not tonight. Your old man is in no shape. Who is this wants to see him?' 'Oh, just someone from around.' Bobby puts up his hand. He'll take care of it. I hope she has enough sense to get him right home."

"Jesus," Kalinyak said, standing. "You know all that happened out there—"

"Stupka said they got it covered, patrols, that sort of thing—"

"Stupka? Man's an asshole. Always was. He says patrols. That means someone drops by the juke joint, has a beer, and drives on. Patrols! We should have never let the daughter—"

"What?"

"Well, the weather out there. This is no night to be driving out there."

"She wouldn't be that stupid," Phil Hanratty said, and downed his drink. Kalinyak hurried out of the bar.

The night was ferocious, a full-fledged storm, icy, granular bursts of snow, piercing wind. He looked for a cab and couldn't find one and ended up walking—jogging actually—back to the hotel where he picked up his car and started for Pine Valley. Inside, he felt a great, sad chill, a hand of fear on his heart. Bobby Mack had asked if he was afraid. He was now.

* * *

The snow was coming down in great, furious gusts, obliterating the road. Bobby Mack's daughter steered his Town Car slowly over the Ninth Street Bridge. She turned onto Federal Street and then Perrysville Avenue. She was now on Route 19 going north toward Pine Valley. Bobby Mack's head was tilted back in the seat, his mouth open; he snored softly.

Lara's eyes were expressionless as she steered through the thick snow. A large green pine tree neon sign came into view. She pulled into the Pine Valley parking lot. She brought the town car to a stop. "Bob. Bob," she said, shaking her father.

He sat up quickly, turned to her, trying to focus. "Where are we?" he said.

"We're going to meet somebody."

"Okay. Okay." He stared at his daughter, looked deeply into her eyes. "Thank you for coming to me. I've missed you."

"I've missed you, too."

"You need some money?" He reached in his pocket and brought out a handful of bills and pressed them on his daughter.

Cory's beaten-up Chevy moved through the snow and parked next to them. The door opened and Marika came out. She held a revolver in her hand.

Lara lowered the window on the driver's side. "Where's Cory?" she said, suddenly very afraid.

"He'll meet you in Pine Valley."

"He promised me—"

"He'll take care of you."

"What is it?" Bobby Mack said, trying to make things clear. Marika motioned with the gun. He looked over at his daughter.

"You'll be all right, Bob. She just wants to talk to you."

Bobby Mack got out of the car and walked with the German girl across the parking lot to the motel next door.

Lara got out of her father's car and hurried into Pine Valley. She was weeping.

* * *

Pine Valley was almost lost in snow as Kalinyak pulled into the lot. He parked next to Bobby Mack's town car. He peered into it. He ran into Pine Valley.

Lara was seated by herself at a small table next to the juke box. There were a half dozen couples seated around. One couple swayed together on the small dance floor. It was the Rolling Stones, "You Can't Always Get What You Want," and the dancers made no effort to follow the music.

Lara looked over at Kalinyak and her face was streaked with tears and her expression was bleak, empty, devastated. "What happened?" Kalinyak said.

"Cory was supposed to meet me. *Filoriandro.* He told me he had doojie. He was going to fix me up." There was a tremor in her voice. "He said he had something for my father—"

"For your father?"

"Information."

"What?"

"About the killings...."

"Where's your father?" She waved in the direction of the motel. "What's he doing there?" Outside there was a muffled sound of a car starting up, then pulling away.

"Cory lied to me, that motherfucker. He lied to me. He never showed."

"What's your father doing at the motel?"

"Marika showed up instead. She came in Cory's car. She had a gun..."

Kalinyak sprinted for the door, Lara behind him. "Is he all right? What is it? What?"

He slipped running across the lot on ice underneath the snow, came down hard on his side, got right up, and continued on to the motel. "Where's the car?" he yelled.

"I don't know. Gone..."

Two doors down from the office, a door was ajar, room number 7. He started inside, then stopped abruptly. Lara came to him. He tried to hold her back, but she pushed right past him.

Her screams shattered the muffled night. "Dear God," Kalinyak said. Her screams continued on and on.

Chapter Seventeen

|||

Kalinyak raced back to town with Lara huddled on the seat next to him. She was sobbing uncontrollably. He called Hanratty at home on his cell. "What? What happened?" Hanratty said, his voice clouded with sleep. "Does Gene Stupka know? That's all right, I'll call him. And the task force?"

"They're there."

"Oh, my God, Kalin..."

He drove through Squirrel Hill. He called Betty Malloy, waking her. He told her he was coming over.

Woodbine Road, leading to Betty's street, hadn't been ploughed yet, and he skidded his way down the hill. At her house, he helped Lisa up the steps. Betty, in a quilted housecoat, opened the door. She looked at Kalinyak and the weeping girl and immediately knew something was wrong. "What is it?"

"Bobby Mack," he said.

"What?"

"He—he—" Kalinyak couldn't pronounce the words.

The color drained from Betty's face. "No..." She gathered Bobby Mack's daughter in her arms. Lisa couldn't stop weeping. Betty held her and tried to comfort her. She cried and cried.

Kalinyak said, "I'll be back later..."

"What are you going to do?" He shrugged, helpless. "Be careful."

He didn't know what he would do and yet he felt he must do something. There had been five of them, great friends in high school, athletes together, the Huns. Four were now dead...

It was after midnight when Kalinyak came to the Aida, inquiring after Cory. The bartender, tidying up behind the bar, seemed bored and uninterested. "Haven't seen him since you were with him earlier," he said.

"I need to talk to him..."

"Well, if I see him..."

Next he went to the Hot Box, then the Strip clubs, the Hard Luck Café, several others. No one had seen Cory for days, the German girl for weeks. A great sense of despair seized Kalinyak.

It was dawn when he returned to Betty Malloy's. She had given Lisa something to calm her down; she was sleeping. Betty was pale, her face tense, stunned. In her eyes, he could see fear. "Have you slept?" he said.

"I can't." She began to weep. "Oh, dear God," she said.

"Who was in charge of contacting people for the reunion?"

"Sally Forrestal. She was on the committee with Doyle. She was in charge of contacting everyone."

"Do you have a number for her?"

"I must have it." She started to look through some papers on a desk and then became flustered, pushed the papers aside. "Oh, where is it?" She took a Pittsburgh phone book out of a drawer. "She's married to Danny Forrestal. Has that flower shop on Murray Avenue. Here it is."

She wrote the number down on a slip of paper and gave it to Kalinyak. He held her. She was trembling. "Oh, God," she said. "Oh, God..."

He drove downtown, parked on Ross Street in front of the great granite courthouse building. He climbed the stone stairs to the DA's office. A half dozen people—detectives, deputy DA's—sat around shattered, confused, in shock. Stupka and Hanratty were there. They looked god-awful. "Mayor's on his way down," Stupka said. "Never seen nothing like this."

"Why did he go out there?" Hanratty said.

"Drunk. You saw him. Daughter said she'd get him some information. Someone used her to set him up. Unless she's involved in this. I don't know. I'm going to take a run back out to Pine Valley. See how they're getting along."

"Kalin, what is this?" Stupka said. "I've never seen nothing like this. Greenfield Bob! Jesus..."

Mayor Brendan Macha arrived just as Kalinyak was coming down the granite stairs in front of the courthouse building. The mayor seemed abstracted as though there were some essential problem he had to solve. "Kalin, I knew him like a brother. All my life I knew him. Little Greenfield Bob. Well, you know. You remember the old days. Who can figure anything in this life?" He shook his head from side to side. There were tears in his eyes.

At Pine Valley, there was nearly a foot of snow in the parking lot, and it was still coming down. The police had set up barriers around the motel area. Flashing his ID, Kalinyak moved past a uniformed cop at the door to room 7 and checked it out. Bobby Mack's body was gone. There was blood everywhere. On the mirror was scrawled in blood, "Baby your out of time." Earlier, he had made a quick survey of the room. He hadn't found an hour glass.

He walked to the motel office and learned from the clerk that a man had paid for the room. "Was there a girl with him?"

"Might have had someone with him in the car. Did glimpse a girl later, blonde, going into the room."

"The man?"

"Different one with the girl. Large, gray-haired. This is the damndest thing. Fourth killing around here. In the seventeen years I've been here, oh, we have had some shootings, some stabbings. Nothing like this."

Kalinyak walked across the parking lot to the club, pushing his way through drifts of snow. Despite the weather and the hour, there were customers, several couples, heavy-set, sloppy early day drinkers. A song played on the juke box.

A rush of memory came over him. He knew the song. He hadn't heard it since—long, long ago. High school!

He remembered it. He remembered the night it played. He remembered what had happened that night.

They had been drinking. It had been buried, buried deep, deep. It came up to him now in all its horror. Chris Farlowe singing a Rolling Stones song. What was it? "Out of Time..."

It had always been with him, that night, that song. He had buried it, but it was always there, a dagger in his soul. When his daughter was killed, he knew it was retribution...

"You don't know what's going on,/You've been away for far too long/ You can't come back and think you are still mine..."

He was back in his car, on his cell phone calling Sally Forrestal. "You contacted the people for the reunion?"

"Yes."

"Sarah Jo Kazmarek?"

"Heard she was dead. Didn't try. Had no information on her."

"Damn..."

"Three weeks before the reunion, she called. She couldn't come to the reunion, but wanted to hear who was coming. She asked about all of you—"

"Who?"

"The Huns. You and Gus Magoczy, Doyle, Bobby Mack. Wanted to know if the Huns were coming..."

"Where was she calling from?"

"She said she lived—where was it? Up north. Oil City."

He sped the distance to Oil City through the snow-heaped countryside. The roads had been ploughed; the shoulders were high with dingy snow. The roadbed was slick, a veneer of slush and black ice. Traveling more than seventy miles an hour, he skidded several times, but managed to keep the car under control.

As he entered the town, he noticed that there were chunks of ice clogging the Allegheny River. He turned down Main Street, past the Petroleum Street Bridge, and followed Relief Street up the hill. The street had only been cleared to where the pavement ended. He noticed foot tracks in the snow leading up to the shack.

The dog rushed the fence, barking furiously, a dark bundle of muscle, incisors dripping slaver, yellow-tinged eyes. "Sarah Jo," Kalinyak called out. "Sarah!"

There was no movement in the shack. The dog continued to snarl and bark. "Sarah. It's Frank Kalin."

The door opened. The old lady stood there watching him. And now he knew her. Through all the wrinkles and the age, the devastation the years had wreaked on her, he could see her. "Hello, Frank," she said.

"Can I come in?"

She stared at him for a long moment. Then she called the dog to her and held him by his chain. He opened the gate and entered the shack.

There was a sitting room with a pot-bellied stove in the center. The walls were flocked with a fading red velvet material. Red shag carpeting covered the floor. An ancient sofa, stuffing spilling from it, and several stuffed chairs completed the décor. "Did you know it was me when I was here the other day?"

"Yes."

"Why didn't you say something?"

"What would I say?"

"It's been a while."

"A long while." She stood there watching him. There was a wariness in her gaze. "What do you want?"

"Where's your son?"

"What do you want with him?"

"Some people you know have been killed." She didn't say anything, just stared at him. He looked at her, and through all the ravages of time and her life, he could see a glimmer of the beauty she had once been. "Where's the girl?"

She shook her head. "She won't let him alone. She comes around. You never know when."

"She looks like you. How you used to look. How is that possible?"

"I don't know what you mean."

He didn't speak for a while. "We did a terrible thing," he said at last. He could barely get the words out. "We had been drinking. For years I never even thought about it. We had been drinking."

She stared at him. When she talked it was with a quiet, girlish voice: "I was a virgin. I was a religious girl. I remember crying out, 'I'm a virgin!'"

"Jack Dahlgren—"

"I was in love with him. He told me we would get married. We were at Pine Valley. I loved that song—"

"'Out of Time...'"

"We played it over and over. He kept giving me drinks. And then you all showed up, the rest of the Huns. And Jack said, 'Rape and pillage...'"

"I had buried it..."

"And you took me to the motel and I would have never believed ... Even Gus Magoczy. I knew all of you from St. Philomena's, from Mirror Street, I knew you since I was four or five years old. I was a good girl, I was a religious girl. The five of you raped me. My life—"

"I'm sorry, Sarah Jo."

"No one ever said anything. Jack Dahlgren laughed about it. I told him I was pregnant and he said—he said—" She was weeping now. "How did he know it was him who was the father? Why not one of you? He called me a whore. He made me into a whore. I was a religious girl..."

"Your son? Cory..."

"Steven..."

"He's—"

"One of you is his father. I don't know which. He had such an unhappy life. He would be in his room back there and I would be up here—and then I would take the men back there, and he'd have to come out here..."

"Why did you go that way?"

"Who could I talk to? My parents threw me out—you know the way they were. They were old school, Iron City. Dad worked in the mill. Mom went to church all the time. She'd take me with her. St. Philomena's. My dad called me a whore. I went to my mother and she screamed at me. I disgraced her. I disgraced the family."

"Where's Steven?"

"I don't know. I haven't seen him in weeks." Kalinyak walked to the door at the side of the room. "Don't go in there..."

"Why?"

"Please, Frank..."

Kalinyak opened the door and walked into her son's room.

Chapter
Eighteen

|||

The room was narrow, done up in red like the front
room. There was a small lamp with a red shade on an end
table, a red silk spread over the bed. Opposite the bed on the
wall was a floor to ceiling mirror on a sliding closet door.
There was a side door leading outside.

Kalinyak looked at the walls and felt his breath rush
from him. They were covered with pictures, newspaper
clippings going back years, about Jack Dahlgren, Doyle
Eggerman, Father Magoczy; there were clippings about
Kalinyak's fight career. And there were souvenirs from high
school—Sarah Jane Kazmarek in bouffant hair, plaid skirt,
saddle shoes, posed with the cheerleading squad. There were
plaques with honors she had won at St. Philomena's and
Allderdice, Most Promising Student, 8th Grade; A Level Choir;
State Debate Tournament, 2nd Place.

Her picture from the high school yearbook had been cut
out and was framed just above the bed. Next to it was a red

cardboard heart with childish crayon scrawl on it: I love you, mother...

There were pictures and souvenirs from Pine Valley. Sarah Jo smiling with Jack Dahlgren. There were photographs of Marika, the German girl made up to look like Sarah Jo.

And there were the most recent pictures, clippings chronicling the murders, photos of Dahlgren, Doyle Eggerman, Father Magoczy. X's had been drawn through them. There was a large photo from years back of the Hunky Hurricane, posed to fight at the Southside Market House. There was no X over Kalinyak's picture.

On the table next to the bed was a 45 rpm record player. The record on it was "Out of Time." He turned it on. The song, crackling with wear, began:

"You don't know what's going on. You've been away for far too long..."

He heard someone behind him. He turned. Sarah Jo stood in the doorway. She spoke so softly he could barely hear her: "It's my fault. I never thought he would do these things. I told him what had happened, over and over, poisoned him with it. What had become of me, was his bedtime story year after year after year. I felt so bad for him and for me. I had no life and he didn't either. You can't blame him, Frank. I tried to tell him it was Dahlgren mainly. The rest of you went along because it was Dahlgren. Gussie tried to stop it, and Dahlgren ridiculed Gus. Creeping Jesus, he called him. He laughed at him.

"We walked from Pine Valley," Sarah Jo said. "We were all drunk. Dahlgren rented a room in the motel. I remember I asked him what was happening. 'You're going to pull a train,' he said."

The sidewall was a closet. Kalinyak slid the door open. There were a number of dresses and several blonde wigs.

"I didn't know what he meant— he pushed me down on the bed and I was crying, 'Please help me. I'm a virgin. Please. Kalin, please...' I was the only thing Stevie had. I poisoned him with it. God forgive me...""

Kalinyak reached out to touch the dresses. He picked up one of the wigs. He saw now, in the mirror, the side door to the room leading outside, open.

Marika stood there, gun in hand.

"No," Sarah Jo said. "No, no..."

"They did terrible things to you," Marika said. "Cory told me all about it."

"Please," Sarah Jo said. "Kalin was always very kind to me..." She walked to Marika and moved to push the gun to one side.

The music from the record player continued on, Chris Farlowe's breathy voice, clicking sounds from the time-worn vinyl disc:

"Well, baby, baby, baby, you're out of time..."

"They ruined you, ruined Stevie's life," Marika said coolly, her blue eyes hard and penetrating... "Cory. He would tell me how lonely he was growing up. How terrible it was to know that his mother was a—was a—"

"No, darling, don't..."

"You're out of time," Marika said to Kalinyak.

He shot her just below the heart, one bullet from Bobby Mack's gun in his jacket pocket. She fell to one side. Her gun clattered on the floor. Sarah Jo knelt next to her and smoothed her hair.

Her eyes stared up at the ceiling. Sarah Jo reached to her eyes and delicately removed the blue contact lenses. Then she removed the blonde wig.

Kalinyak saw on a nightstand something groomed, expensive. He held it up to his face, looked at himself in the mirror. It was a prop moustache, Cory's moustache.

Marika, of course, was Sarah Jo's son.

She didn't weep. She sat on the floor next to her son and cradled him in her arms. She looked up at Kalinyak. "It was my fault, God forgive me. Jesus forgive me. I did terrible things to him. He was so lost as a child. He had no one. He invented someone to play with. He became me..."

"Dahlgren did terrible things," Kalinyak said. "We all did. The Huns. Rape and pillage."

He felt now a great sob well up in him, choking his heart, a monumental despair. With Dahlgren and the others, the Five Huns, he had raped Sarah Jo Kazmarek. That act that night so many years ago had dogged his life, corroded everything he had ever done. He had fought to bury it, wipe it out. All the energy it had taken to push it down, bury it! He couldn't, of course. No way. It would come to him at odd terrible times, come to him in dreams, when he was alone, showering, listening to music; when he was with people, at parties, at the movies, watching sports. It haunted his marriage, his relationship to his daughter. With her murder it had overwhelmed him; he was wracked with the knowledge of what he had done. He was to blame! Her death was retribution!

He had died with his daughter. He was buried with his daughter. And what he had done was buried with both of them.

But of course it wasn't.

"I forgive you," Sarah Jo said. "*God the Father of Heaven, have mercy on us. God the Son, Redeemer of the world, have mercy on us. God the Holy Ghost, have mercy on us. Holy Trinity one God, have mercy on us. Holy Mary, Queen of Virgins, St. Philomena, pray for us...*"

Chris Farlowe sang:

> *You're obsolete, my baby*
> *My poor old fashioned baby...*

The record came to an end. The needle scratched on the vinyl. The player clicked off.

Kalinyak had never in his life felt so desolate, not even at the death of his daughter.

Epilogue

Kalinyak knew two things: he would have to give up booze and cigarettes again. And he would have to find a life for himself.

After phoning Hanratty and telling him what had happened, he returned to the hotel.

He would have to stay around until everything was resolved, he was aware of that, but he didn't want to remain at the hotel. He began to pack his bags. He gathered up the pictures of his daughter. He stared a long time at her. He kissed her picture. Then he drove to Betty Malloy's.

Lisa and Betty sat in the kitchen having breakfast. "Sit," Betty said.

"I can't stay. I have to meet with the people downtown." He told them what happened, of the madness of Cory, of Sarah Jo Kazmarek. He told them about the rape so many years before.

No one spoke for a long while.

"Where are you going to go now?" Betty said. He shook his head, shrugged. "Why don't you stay here, Frank?"

Kalinyak stood in the kitchen, tired, drained. What would he do? Where would he go?

"Sit down, Frank. Have some breakfast," Betty said. "Lisa and I have been talking."

"I might stay here, too" Lisa said. "See if I can kick."

"You need a family, Frankie Kalin," Betty said. She broke some eggs, beat them in a bowl, and poured them into a frying pan.

"We could be a family," Lisa said.

In his mind's eye, Frank Kalinyak saw Pine Valley and the Huns and Sarah Jo. He saw them walking toward the motel. He heard the song echoing in his mind, *"Baby, you're out of time..."*

Something stirred in him, a glimmer within him. A family, he thought. A family.

Yes, maybe it could be. Maybe they could be a family.

Acknowledgements

I would like to thank Christopher Meeks for his unfailing encouragement and an exquisite editorial eye that more than once saved me from authorial embarrassment, repeating a funeral, switching a name in mid-book, deploying exclamation points like confetti, stuff that I find maddening in others, but eccentric and endearing when I do it.

Thanks also to Carol Fuchs, whose assiduous and discerning copy edit attempted to make sure all the commas, periods, colons, semi-colons, and quotation marks were properly placed in face of a writers' irritating penchant for grammatical exotica.

To Kiran Sethi, a lady of incomparable taste and abilities, an artist and world-class educator, whose book design for this volume and my earlier novel, "The Fat Lady Sings," faithfully mirrored the authors' intent.

And to Abby Milton, thanks for making sure the whole thing made sense, and for keeping her father from overdosing on pizza and banana splits.

About the Author

David Scott Milton was an early member of Theater Genesis in New York alongside Sam Shepard, Leonard Melfi, and Murray Mednick. His first plays, *The Interrogation Room* and *Halloween Mask,* were produced there. Later plays, *Duet* and *Bread,* were done at the American Place Theatre. *Duet,* starring Ben Gazzara, went on to Broadway. Milton's play *Skin* won the Neil Simon Playwriting Award.

His screenplay, *Born to Win,* became Ivan Passer's first American film and starred George Segal and Karen Black. He has published six novels. *Paradise Road,* was cited by the Mark Twain Journal "for significant contribution to American literature."

From 1977 until 2011, he taught playwriting and screenwriting at the University of Southern California. For thirteen years, he taught creative writing at the maximum security prison in Tehachapi, California. A dramatic piece he created about his prison experiences, *Murderers Are My Life,* was nominated as best one-man show by the Valley Theater League of Los Angeles.

Visit the website: www.dsmilton.com
or **www.WhiteWhiskerBooks.com**